I Should'a Been a Cowboy

D.L. Bjorngjeld

Published by Dennis L. Bjorngjeld
Forest Lake, Minnesota

ISBN 978-0-9981110-0-1

Layout & Design by Todd Anderson

Sketches by D. L. Bjorngjeld

Printed in United States of America

Preface

I've lived nearly all of my 70 years in Anoka County, Minnesota. In younger years, my heroes were the great cowboys like Roy Rogers, Gene Autry, Hopalong Cassidy, and others. Through the 50s and early 60s, we'd watch them on TV, and spend many Saturday afternoons watching them at our small town theatre. For over 20 years I enjoyed my own horses. On Saturdays, my family, and several neighboring families, would load up our horses. Then, with coolers of food and beverage, we'd head for one of the Western Gaming shows at local arenas. There we would enjoy picnicking, while everyone rode in the various events, even picking up a blue ribbon or two.

As I continued my writing efforts – making a number of attempts at producing a good novel – I finally decided to follow an old adage and write about something I really love... Cowboys and the old west.

A thousand thank yous   to my sister, Karen Bjorngjeld - Savelkoul. She's a voracious reader, and her professional background as a proofreader was a great help from start to finish. Thank you Sis!

Chapter One

"On the floor!" I whispered to my wife and son, holding back the panic that I felt. "Quick, on the floor!"

I grabbed Reagan, the youngest of our three sons, held a finger to his lips for him to stay quiet, then gently forced him to the floor next to Sonja. She drew him into her arms, holding her finger to his lips and trying to give him a smile. When she glanced up at me, fear was etched on her face. "Please be careful, Mack," she whispered.

"I will," I mouthed, and forced a smile. With a gentle squeeze of her shoulder, I rose to see who was there... who had shouted, "Put the money in this bag... *NOW*!"

Peeking over and around the stacked grocery items, I saw a guy holding a gun aimed at the clerk. I thought, *Who is this guy? Zorro?* He wore a black cloth with holes cut for his eyes. It covered his head, and was tied in the back.

Shakily pointing his gun at the clerk, he looked edgy and nervous. It seemed like the least little thing could set him off on a shooting spree. I needed to move before that happened. I reached back for the Colt Defender that I carry in a concealment holster, while thinking about what I could do to get his attention away from the clerk.

With the Colt in hand, I picked up a loaf of bread, and held it by the bag so it would hide the gun. Then, quietly opening the cooler door, I grabbed a half gallon of milk from the shelf. Letting the door close loudly, I stepped around the end of the grocery shelf shouting, "Say... have you got any gallon jugs of this brand of..."

"Hey!" the startled gunman yelled, swinging his gun toward me.

I slowly raised my hands, one holding the milk, the other the loaf of bread with the gun hidden behind it. "Easy buddy... take it easy. I ain't gonna give you no trouble."

"Git down on the floor!" he shouted. "Now! Do it!"

"Okay... okay..." I said shakily, trying to sound nervous. As I began to crouch, the gunman quickly turned and fired a shot toward the clerk. I threw the milk and bread to my left, then dove and rolled to the right. I came up on one knee and fired two quick rounds, hitting the gunman twice in the chest. He had a surprised, deer-in-the-headlights look, glanced down at his chest, then collapsed to the floor.

Getting to my feet, I heard the clerk yell, "Look out!" Behind the front shelves of merchandise was another gunman who had been standing watch at the window. I saw a gun ease it's way around the end of a shelf, then the guy attached to it quickly peered out and fired two rounds my way. The explosion of sound slapped my ears, then I flinched when I felt a burning pain tear through my left side. I raised my Colt and fired two rounds in return, hit him and saw him begin to fall.

On the way down he fired again, and I felt like I'd been hit on the side of the head with a baseball bat. Everything went black and I collapsed, hitting the floor hard.

For an instant, my senses went numb and silence filled the store. After what seemed like a long while, I heard Sonja's footsteps rushing to me. At the same time she was shouting to the clerk. "Call 9-1-1. Hurry! Tell them an officer is down."

2

Through the thick fog in my head, I could hear the clerk hitting the buttons on his phone and frantically talking to someone. At the same time, I heard Sonja softly saying, "Mack... Mack..." and felt her fingers pressing firmly on my neck. After a long pause, she whispered, "Thank God!"

I heard Reagan's footsteps, then his small voice asking, "Daddy?" I wanted to console him and tell him I was going to be fine, but I couldn't move or make a sound.

Sonja reached out her arm and waved him to her. Holding him close, she said, "It's gonna be okay, baby. Daddy's gonna be okay."

Later, lying on an emergency room bed, I still hadn't regained consciousness... to the rest of the world anyway. My vital signs were good and strong, but Sonja found it unnerving that I was still in a coma-like state. For the third time, she asked, "Why is he still unconscious?"

The doctor sounded consoling, saying, "I know this is upsetting, but everything looks good with your husband."

He gave some instructions to a nurse, then continued with Sonja. "I'm convinced the bullet to his head, even though it only scratched his skull, caused enough trauma to knock him unconscious. We're more concerned about the internal bleeding from his other gunshot wound right now, but it's not life threatening and we'll have him in surgery as soon as we feel it's safe for him."

"I'm sorry doctor," I heard her say. "I know you're on top of things. It's just that...." She stopped, and I could hear her soft sobbing.

"No need to apologize, Mrs. MacAlan. I know this is agonizing for you right now."

3

"It's our second time around with him being shot," she said, sniffling.

Why are they talking about me this way, I wondered. Then I tried to speak, saying, *I'm gonna be okay, Sonny.* Sonny is Sonja's nickname. But I soon realized that my attempt to speak was nothing more than a thought passing through my foggy brain.

I tried again. *Sonny, I'm okay... everything's gonna be okay.* I laid there puzzled, wondering what was going on. *Except for the throbbing in my head, I feel okay. Why won't things work?*

Then I thought I'd try to slap the bed. Maybe I could get their attention... somehow let them know I'm okay. My brain told my hand to rise up and slap down hard, but nothing happened. There was only a numb, helpless sensation that was extremely frustrating.

I lay there for a while, then finally realized that nothing was working. *My eyes*, I thought. *My eyes won't open! Why can't I open them?*

I tried to remain calm. Finally, I thought, *Is this what being dead feels like?*

Chapter Two

I laid there motionless... still puzzled... still frustrated. *This can't be death*, I told myself. Suddenly, I had the strange sensation of being pulled from my body. Like a space shuttle anchored to a huge rocket, I was leaving the launching pad and felt the crushing pressure of the sudden upward thrust. I could see the hospital room shrinking below, then everything turned white in a blur of blinding light and an explosion of speed. I was accelerating through space and time, not knowing how or why. The heart-stopping explosion of speed was completely out of my control. I was at it's mercy, as it bent light and distorted dimensions.

Suddenly, it seemed as though I snapped through a wrinkle in time, and was catapulted into the past. Things suddenly shifted into slow motion, and I was standing in a sagebrush landscape somewhere in the old west. As my head cleared, I was staring at endless open range. In the distance, rock formations jutted skyward, and sage-covered hills rolled up against high buttes. I felt a gentle breeze that carried the fresh breath of sage.

I raised my hand to shade my eyes, and squinted at a group of buildings silhouetted against the western horizon. The hills beyond were lit by the golden glow of the early sun that was inching over the eastern horizon. The sun warmed my back, and painted the landscape with bright, rich hues.

I reached up for my hat and paused, hand in mid-air. *Hat?* I thought, and removed a tan Stetson from my head. It was dusty, and had a darkened sweat-stain around the band. I brushed away the dust, stared at it for a moment, then put it back on my head, surprised at how familiar it felt.

A bit puzzled, I shifted my weight and rested my hand on my gun. *Gun?* I was more than a little surprised, startled even, when I looked down and saw a well-worn leather holster hanging on my hip, and my hand resting on the butt of a six-gun. Drawing it from the holster, I looked at a .45 caliber Colt Peacemaker, with a five-and-a-half-inch barrel. From reading I'd done in my fascination with the old west and cowboys, I seemed to remember that gunslingers preferred shorter barrels, like the five-and-a-half-inch, for easier handling and speed. I examined the Colt, gently stroking it with my fingertips. As I slid it back into the holster, I noticed how natural and fluid the motion felt.

Still staring down at the Peacemaker hanging on my hip, I whispered, "A gunslinger? Me? Can't be."

I lifted the gun once again, feeling its weight in my hand, then dropped it back into its holster. I shifted my feet, spreading them slightly, and drew the gun quickly. The motion was instinctive... and lightning fast. As my thumb pulled back on the hammer, my hand gripped and drew the gun. It was so quick and fluid that it surprised me.

"Whoa!" I whispered, as I stared down at the gun.

I eased it back in the holster, relaxed my hand, then drew again. I pulled the hammer back to half-cock, and flipped open the loading gate to check the cylinder. There were five cartridges, with the hammer resting on the empty chamber. I slid the Colt back in the holster and spoke to it, saying, "Well, let's see how well you shoot."

I glanced around, picked up a rock about the size of my fist, and walked to a large bush that had a dead branch. I rested the rock on the fork of three dead offshoots, then walked twenty-five or thirty feet away.

Not wanting to give it much thought, I drew and fired. The Colt barked loudly, and kicked against my hand. The bark and kick hadn't surprised me... I'd been ready for it. What did surprise me, was the big puff of powder that exploded off the rock as it flew from the branch.

Wondering how it was at rapid fire, I glanced at the dead branch, pointed the Colt with the trigger held back, then fanned the hammer with the heel of my left hand. Four shots fired quickly, and splinters flew from the thick branch with each shot. *Nice to know what you can do... if need be,* I thought.

I leaned down to brush away the dust from my Levis. They were well-worn, and had three-inch cuffs rolled up at the bottom. The cuffs hung over leather boots that were old, scuffed, and very comfortable. From the pocket of my leather vest, I pulled out a gold, hunter-case watch and opened the spring-hinged lid. The watch showed six-fifteen and, from the location of the sun, that seemed about right. As I clicked the watch closed and slipped it back into the vest pocket, I heard the soft knicker of a horse.

I turned to see a beautiful young mare with a shiny black coat, four white socks, and a white blaze on her forehead. She had a finely shaped head, and perky ears. I moved closer, studying the white blaze running between her intelligent eyes. "Hey there, Blaze. How are you, girl?" I said softly. Blaze seemed like a good name.

She bobbed her head, then gently nudged me in the chest. I moved to check the cinch on the saddle, and found it snugged up tight. With a hop and a pull on the saddle horn, I stuck a boot in the stirrup and swung my leg over. She raised her head slightly, pranced a little, then calmed.

I leaned forward, patting her on the side of her neck and scratching her cheek. "Good girl, Blaze. Let's take a ride and see what that town over yonder is all about." She blew loudly, and shook a fly from her ear.

With subtle pressure from my legs, she moved ahead at a nice walk. We'd gone only a short way, when she bobbed her head and hesitated. From behind I heard panting breath and padded feet. I turned in the saddle and saw a large, black dog coming. "So, where did you come from big guy?" I asked.

I swung down and, when I knelt to pet him, he immediately sat in front of me. He was big and strong, with a large handsome head. He had a smooth, shiny black coat, and a small white patch on his neck just below his jaw. "I guess you'll have to be 'Patch'," I told him, scratching all around his ears and neck.

I finally stood, considering them both. "Blaze and Patch..." I said, "my new best friends."

I swung back in the saddle, and the three of us headed west toward the distant town. Rocking with Blaze's rhythm, I relaxed and watched Patch playfully circle us as we moved along. I curiously scanned the far-reaching, rolling prairie of sagebrush and scrub trees. Interesting rock formations reached skyward, and high buttes blended into rolling mountains. The immense landscape drew my eye out farther and farther until, at the horizon, purple-gray sagebrush touched clear blue sky.

The only movement I saw was the lazy drift of a soft, fluffy cloud.

Chapter Three

As I scanned the immense range, my thoughts drifted to something deep inside... distant memories. Sonja and my intense love for her. Our sons, Jacob and Max, who were only a year from college. And Reagan, our youngest, with a dozen years of living and growing before thinking about college.

Of the three, only Reagan shared my enthusiasm for cowboys and the old west. Most days, you'd see him wearing his big red, ten gallon hat (a little skewed), black cowboy boots (a little floppy), and pearl handle six guns (all plastic).

He was always ready to ride. We were Texas Rangers chasing down bad guys and their gangs. The likes of John Wesley Hardin, Wild Bill Longley, Jesse James, or some other nasty desperado was our target. Reagan's horse was a Palomino named Lucky, and mine was a Line-Back Dun named Nikki.

I'd been a police officer for nine years, and was discharged on full disability after being injured in a gunfight my partner and I had with drug dealers. Through the years I'd been fascinated with the old west, and had read a great deal about it. I loved the romanticized view of that rugged life, where men were men, and the good guys always won. Like most, I avoided the reality of the desperate, hard-scrabble life that it really was.

I had a collection of guns, including a fine Colt Peacemaker from the late 1800's. Reagan loved to watch me practice my quick draw. But respect for, and safety with guns was always foremost with my family.

Sonja mostly tolerated our cowboy antics, sometimes saying things like, "You two Rangers gonna climb down from your horses and give 'em a rest? Maybe do some work in the yard today?"

Reagan was getting pretty sharp with his comebacks. "Miss Sonja," he'd drawl, "us Rangers got way too much 'portant stuff to take care of. No time to bother with things like yard work."

I'd quickly steer him toward the garage, throwing Sonja a grin and telling Reagan, "We better git to work, pod'ner, else Miss Sonja's liable to yank our badges."

Chapter Four

I saw a road, and my mind came back to the range. Actually, it was just a rutted trail, worn down through the years by buggies, wagons and stagecoaches. As we neared the town, I saw a corral attached to a big barn. There were several horses in the corral, and some buggies by the barn. A sign above the wide double-doors read, "Big Jake's Livery and Blacksmith."

Across the street, was a freshly painted white church, with a sign that read, "Eagle Bluff Christian Church." Its tall steeple housed a pair of large bells. Above the wide front entry, there was a beautiful stained-glass window. Behind the church, a small cemetery was surrounded by a white picket fence.

The street headed west through town for three blocks, then turned left and went south. Buildings lined each side of the street, and a boardwalk ran in front of the businesses and shops that occupied the buildings. At the corner there was a large L-shaped building that wrapped around the outside of the corner. It had an angled double-door entry in the middle. Above the tall, heavy doors, a wide sign with bold, red lettering said, "Eagle Bluff Hotel, Diner and Saloon."

"Well, Blaze," I said, walking her to the hitching rack in front of the hotel, "I think we've found ourselves in the fine town of Eagle Bluff." I swung from the saddle, and wrapped the reins on the rail.

"Patch, you'd better stay here with Blaze," I told him. He laid down on the boardwalk, and glanced up as though checking that she was alright.

11

"Good boy," I said, patting him as I stepped onto the boardwalk. His head lifted and his ears twitched, liking the attention.

I walked in the open double doors, and paused. Coming from the bright morning sun into the darker entry, I waited for my eyes to adjust. In moments, I looked around. To my right, was a door marked "Diner." Across from that, on the left, swinging doors gave way to the Saloon. Ahead, there was a large lobby and hotel registration desk.

Everything looked well-crafted and very impressive. I glanced around, taking it all in, and noticed someone standing behind the wide registration desk. He appeared to be the hotel's clerk, or maybe the owner — I didn't know which. And it seemed that he liked a dapper look, or featured himself far more appealing to the ladies than he likely was — again, I didn't know which.

He wore a fancy, ruffled white shirt, black tie, and a black vest. He was a little overweight, and had a full, round face. His short hair was parted in the middle, with swooping curls spreading on his forehead that seemed to accentuate the roundness of his face.

"Howdy stranger," he said, smiling. "Welcome to Eagle Bluff." Offering his hand, he added, "My name is Patrick Kennedy. But, please, call me Pat. I'm the proprietor of this fine hotel."

I reached to shake his hand. "Hello Pat. My name's Troy MacAlan. Most call me Mack."

"Just ride in this morning, Mack?"

"Yes... I did."

"Here on business, or just passin' through?"

"Not sure. Thought I'd just be passin' through, but it seems nice here, and mighty welcoming."

"It is," he said, puffing his chest a little. "We take great pride in our town. But... we don't put up with trouble-makers."

I raised my hands in front of me, saying, "No need to worry. You'll get no trouble from me. No sir."

"That's good to know. Are you lookin' for a room?"

"Well, what's your rate?"

"A room for the night is fifty-five cents. A room with three meals in our diner is ninety-five cents."

"Sounds fair enough. I'll have the full menu for one day, while I decide if I'm staying longer." I reached in my pocket, brought out a silver dollar and laid it on the counter. Turning the registration book toward me, he asked me to sign it. Then, giving me the key for Room 27 and a nickle in change, he wrote the room number next to my name.

"It's at the top of the stairs, down the hall on the right," he said.

"Thanks, Pat." I thumbed my hat, and decided to stop in the Diner for the first of my three meals. As I relaxed, drinking coffee and eating a good breakfast, I was thinking about the silver dollar I'd given Pat. I was surprised to find it when I reached in my pocket. *Better take inventory... see just what I've got,* I thought.

Chapter Five

I finished my breakfast, and stepped out onto the boardwalk. *Inventory*, I thought. First I checked my pants pockets. In one I found two more silver dollars, a ten dollar gold piece, and some smaller change. In the other, I found a jackknife. In my shirt pocket were several wooden matches.

I knew the gold watch was in my left vest pocket. I lifted the flap covering the right vest pocket, and found three twenty-dollar gold pieces. "Hmm, we're pretty well healed," I told Patch, as I stared at the double eagles.

He was on his feet with his head tilted, curious about just what I was doing. I reached down, scratched his neck and patted him on the shoulder. "We're in good shape, "I told him. He looked puzzled.

I stepped down from the boardwalk to check the saddle. Tied behind it, was a bedroll with a ground sheet, a blanket, and a rain slicker. A hand-carved leather scabbard held a Model 1866 Spencer, .50 caliber rifle. It's a fine piece, and was full of cartridges.

I slipped the rifle back into the scabbard, and opened one of the saddlebags, where I found a small cook kit and a canteen full of water. I stepped around Blaze, patting her rump, and opened the other saddlebag. There was a pouch of jerked beef, so I took out a piece and bit off a small chunk. *Mmmm, pretty good*, I thought.

Returning the pouch, I saw two boxes of bullets... one each for the Colt and Spencer. Then I found another pouch that was made of rough leather, and seemed kind of hefty. I lifted it out of the saddlebag, and opened the drawstring.

15

Looking in the pouch, I froze for a moment, my eyes wide. The pouch was half full of small gold nuggets. *Man, oh man, this must be worth hundreds, maybe thousands.* I hefted the pouch again, feeling its weight, then re-tied the drawstring and put it back in the saddlebag.

"Nice to know just what we've got," I said to Patch and Blaze... and to myself.

I took the reins from the rail, stuck my foot in the stirrup, and swung up in the saddle. "Whadaya think guys, should we have a look at more of this town?"

With no answer, I shrugged, reigned Blaze around, and we moseyed down the other leg of their main street. I was impressed with the number of businesses and shops on both sides of the street. We passed the "Eagle Bluff Gazette," and through the glass I could see their large printing press. Sitting at a wide desk, was a man I guessed to be the editor or publisher of the local paper.

Next to the Gazette, was the "Dusty Eagle Saloon." The heavy outside doors that are locked up at closing, were not yet opened to expose the swinging doors that give way to the saloon. Through the window, I could see someone mopping the floor, getting things ready for the day's business.

A couple doors down the line, I saw "Jeff's Guns and Ammunition" and thought, *Now I know where to get ammo if I need it.* A fellow, probably Jeff, swung the shop's door wide, set a tarnished brass spittoon to hold it open, then waved, saying, "Good morning."

"Mornin'," I said, thumbing my hat brim.

Across the street, I saw "Myron's Barber Shop." The familiar candy-striped pole stood next to the door. In front of the shop was a hitching rail and trough of water. Earlier, I had caught a glimpse of myself in the hotel mirror, and thought I could use a shave and a haircut. I eased Blaze toward the trough, then swung down from the saddle, lowered the reins and let her drink. Pointing to the stairway, I said, "Up here, Patch." From there he could drink, too.

When they'd both drank their fill, I moved Blaze to the hitching rail and wrapped the reins. "Patch, you stay here with Blaze," I said, pointing at the boardwalk in front of the rail. As before, he turned to lay down and glanced up at Blaze.

When I swung the door open, a tiny bell mounted just above the door tinkled, then tinkled again as I closed it. A man stepped from the back room, wiping his mouth as though he'd been eating his breakfast. "Hi there, stranger," he said. "How're you this mornin'?"

"I'm doin' fine."

"Here for a shave, a cut, or both?"

"Both," I answered, stroking my chin.

"Well, climb in," he said, pointing to the chair.

I hung my hat on one of the pegs mounted in a row on the wall, and stepped toward the chair. Behind it, was an impressive wall of pine cabinetry. The center space was filled with a large mirror. On each side, was a series of shelves that held a large collection of soap cups and brushes, each one with a different design and color. The center shelf, across the bottom of the mirror, held eight straight razors, all with unique inlaid handles.

"Nice collection," I said, pointing to the shelves.

"Thanks. Been at this for fifty years, so I've managed to collect some trinkets." He was lean, with a full head of wavy hair, and a handsome look.

"More than trinkets," I said, climbing in the chair. "I expect they're more like treasures and memories."

"Nice of you to recognize that," he said, giving his large cloth a good shake to the side before draping it over me. Reaching for a pitcher of hot water that sat on the shelf behind him, he poured some in a basin and put a clean towel in the hot water. After gingerly ringing out the towel, he draped it over my face. I flinched slightly, but in a few seconds the heat felt good on my face. Soon, he removed the towel and painted my face with a soap brush.

Next, he grabbed a heavy strap hanging from the chair and stroked one of the razors back and forth, honing the edge until he was satisfied with its sharpness. He began shaving my face and neck, and said, "Can't say that I recognize your face, been in town long?"

"Nope. Just came in this morning."

"Stayin' long?"

"Not sure. Thought I'd be passing through, but you've got a nice town here, and I'm gonna stay the night. I'll check things out more tomorrow. Who knows?"

"So, you got a room at the hotel?" he asked.

"Yeah, just for tonight."

"Met Pat, did ya?"

"Yeah. Seems like a nice enough sort of guy."

He hesitated, then said, "Sort of... I guess."

I could tell it wasn't a vote of confidence, or any kind of praise, but thought I'd let it rest for the moment. As he finished the shave, wiped my face and neck clean, and got ready to trim my hair, I thought maybe I'd get my nose into it a little more.

"That Pat over at the hotel," I said, "is he the kind who smiles and glad-hands you to your face, then might do differently behind your back."

After a pause, he said, "Mighty perceptive."

I let the subject be. Who knows, maybe I'll decide to hang around this town for a while, and will have reason to know more.

He finished cutting my hair, removed the barber's cloth, and began brushing away hair trimmings. Finally, rechecking to be sure he'd finished with everything, he splashed some nice smelling lotion into his hands and, from behind, lightly patted my face and neck.

"There you go," he told me, spinning the chair so I could have a good look.

I turned my head side to side, looking in the big mirror. "Hey, I clean up pretty good." I slid from the chair and, as I brushed hair from my pants, asked, "How much do I owe you, Myron?"

"A dime for the shave, plus fifteen for the hair cut... twenty-five cents total."

I fished out two dimes and a nickle, and handed them to him with, "Thanks, Myron. Thanks a lot." I stepped toward the wall, and reached for my hat.

He smiled, holding the coins up between his thumb and forefinger. "Thank you..." he said, then hesitated, deep in thought. "I guess I didn't get your name when you came in. Or did I?"

"No, I don't remember giving it. I'm Troy MacAlan. They call me Mack."

"Well thanks, Mack. Hope to see you again."

"Oh, I'm sure you will, Myron," I said, then heard the tinkle of the bell as I opened the door.

Chapter Six

I left Myron's, and stood on the boardwalk feeling fresh and clean. Patch came closer, sniffing curiously, and wondering about the new smell. "It's okay Patch. It's just some smelly face stuff," I told him, and scratched his head. I stretched, looking up and down the boardwalk. "Think I'm gonna take a stroll, Patch." I stuck my head back in Myron's, asking, "Okay if I leave my dog and horse here, while I take a stroll around town?"

"Sure. Glad to keep an eye on 'em," he said, nodding. "They'll be safe and sound."

"Thanks, Myron. I know they'll be in good hands with you here looking out for 'em." I thumbed my hat, and returned his bright, friendly smile.

I walked to the newspaper office, hoping I could get a copy of their latest paper and learn more about the town. Opening the door, I said, "Hi there, my name's Mack," and nodded toward the man behind a desk

"Hello, I'm Dave Long," the man replied, standing to shake my hand. He was slightly shorter than me, with a strong, stocky build. He seemed to have a genuine friendliness about him, and showed a broad smile.

"You the owner?" I asked.

"Nope. Editor. Sean Kennedy is the owner."

"Kennedy? Related to Pat at the hotel?" I asked.

"Brothers," he said, seeming less than pleasant.

21

"O-h-h-h..." I said, stretching it out, and lifting my head in acknowledgment. "But as the editor, you must run the paper."

"Well, I'm reporter, writer, editor, and pressman... so I do put the paper together. But Sean calls the shots on what we print... and what we don't."

This was beginning to stir my curiosity. Why were they, the Kennedy family, so disliked? Like before, I thought I'd let it rest. "I was hoping to get a copy of your latest paper. Maybe learn a little about Eagle Bluff."

He took one from a stack on the corner of his desk, saying, "This week's edition. Just came out yesterday. It's on the house."

"Thanks Dave. I appreciate it."

"You fixin' to stay a while?" he asked.

"Not sure yet... maybe if I can find work."

"Well, there's ranch work available in the area, and a couple of the businesses in town are lookin' for help, too."

"I'll have to check those things out," I told him. Then turning and waving the paper, I added, "Thanks again for this."

"You bet. Let me know if I can help with more."

I stopped next at Jeff's Gun Shop, where I found him busy dusting and arranging his merchandise. "Come on in!" he said cheerfully, as he set his rag down and brushed his hands together.

"Don't stop on my account," I told him. "I'm just nosing around town, checking things out."

"Help your self to a look around," he offered, as he picked up his rag again. "I see you carry a Colt on your hip. Do you own a rifle?"

"An 1866 Spencer."

"That's a good piece. You're well equipped."

"Are you a gunsmith, too?" I asked. "In case anything needs to be worked on?"

"Yep. I can fix just about anything that shoots."

"Good to know. It looks like you carry most every kind of ammunition, too."

"Most of it... definitely everything you need for the Colt and the Spencer." He went back to his dusting and organizing while I browsed, admiring his impressive display of pistols and rifles.

After a time, I moved toward the door, ready to leave. "Thanks. I'll be back when I'm low on ammo."

"Good!" he replied. "Say, I didn't get your name."

"Troy MacAlan. Call me Mack."

"Okay Mack. You've probably already guessed that I'm Jeff... Jeff Koul." He noticed my glance at the injuries and burn scars on his hands, arms and face. Then, without the slightest self-consciousness or self-pity, he brushed an arm saying, "Unpleasant reminders of Gettysburg."

"North or South?"

"I fought under General G.K. Warren of the Union Army. I was injured at Little Round Top."

I gave him a brief smile, then said, "God bless you Mr. Koul. You paid a steep price."

"A price I'd pay again, if it'd help in the cause of saving our nation," he told me proudly.

Changing the subject, I asked, "You wouldn't know any ranchers that are lookin' for help?"

"Will Witten, three miles west of town, is lookin' for a new hand." He paused, "Oh, and I think Adam Kennedy. His ranch is a few miles south of town, and he was lookin' for help recently."

Another Kennedy? I was going to let it go, but instead decided to ask, "Is he any relation to Sean and Patrick Kennedy?"

Giving me a long, measuring look, he asked, "You know them?"

"No. I met Pat at the hotel, and Dave over at the paper told me about Sean."

He paused again, then said, "Adam's another brother. They and their father own a good chunk of this town and area. Problem is... sometimes they seem to act like they run the whole darn place."

I picked up a nice looking jackknife from a display near the door. Studying it, I said, "That kind of thing doesn't make for the best of situations."

"Don't get me wrong, Mack. Our people and our town are great. The Kennedys just manage to keep the tension level turned up."

"Guess I've known those kind," I said, and set the knife back on the display. "Well... thanks for your time Jeff. See you again."

"Have a good day," he replied, waving.

I walked back to the barbershop, and opened the door. Myron was sitting in his chair reading the paper, and looked up when he heard the bell. "Thanks for keeping an eye on 'em for me, Myron."

"Any time. Come back again."

Back out on the boardwalk, I scratched Patch's back, then stepped down to unwrap the reins from the hitching rail. I lifted them over Blaze's head, saying, "Time we check out the livery stable, and get you a room for the night."

As we rode up to Big Jakes, I saw a large man that I figured must be Jake. He was bent over, nailing a shoe to a horse's hoof. He lowered the horse's leg, stood to stretch his back, then said, "Hello there!"

The name 'Big Jake' suited him well. I'm six feet tall and a hundred-ninety pounds. He had to be six foot-five and two hundred-ninety pounds. He had a neck like a tree stump, massive shoulders, and huge bear-paw-like hands.

I thumbed my hat, saying, "Hello Jake. I'm Mack."

"My pleasure... Mack you said?"

"Actually, it's Troy MacAlan. Folks call me Mack."

25

He moved to lay his tools on a large anvil asking, "What can I help you with, Mack?" As he waited for my answer, he picked up a rag to wipe the sweat from his face, then wiped his hands.

"I wanted to stable my horse for a day or two."

"Sure. It's ten cents a day in the pasture, and five cents more in a stall overnight, with grain and hay."

"Let's pamper her with the full treatment. It'll be day by day, until I decide if I'm moving on or not. I'm hoping to find some ranch work." I handed him fifteen cents, and asked, "Do you know Will Witten? I hear he might be hiring."

"Sure do. He stopped here earlier this morning."

"Is he still in town?"

"Yeah. Said he was gonna have lunch at Kristine's, then head for home."

I remembered seeing Kristine's Eatery two doors down from Myron's. "Thanks Jake," I said. "Come on, Patch, let's take a walk to the Eatery."

At Kristine's, I stepped in the open door, and the air was filled with the delicious smell of fried chicken, fresh coffee and baked bread. A potbelly stove sat in the center of the room, surrounded by tables covered in red and white checkered cloth.

Kristine seemed to have a knack for decorating. On the walls were several nice paintings, and on every table was a small vase holding daisies. The tables were nearly all filled, and I took the only one available.

26

A waitress, with pretty eyes and a sweet smile, saw me sit down and walked over. I asked her name. She said it was Whitney, and asked if I wanted a cup of coffee.

"Yes I do," I answered. "And could you tell me if Will Witten is here today?"

She smiled, and pointed to a table in the far corner. "That's him in the dark blue shirt, with the other three gentlemen over there."

"Okay... thanks. Don't bother him right now. I'll catch him before he leaves."

I was eating a tasty chicken and mashed potato dinner, and reading the paper from Dave. I noticed the date and stopped. It said Thursday, May 20, 1880. *Interesting*.

A while later, Witten's group was standing to leave. As he walked by, I asked, "Excuse me, are you Will Witten?"

"Yes... I am." He paused to look me over, then asked, "Why do you ask?"

He was lean, with broad shoulders and strong hands from many years of ranch work. He had a rugged, handsome look. His hair was dark brown and combed back. I guessed him to be five-eleven, a hundred-seventy pounds. Waiting until he was outside before putting on his hat, told me he was a reasonable man, with good manners.

"I was wondering if you're looking for a hired hand. Make that, I was hoping you're looking for one," I said.

"Well, if you don't mind workin' on fence lines, I've got a couple weeks of that. Then maybe a few more things when that's done."

27

"Don't mind fencing at all," I told him.

"Do you know where I live?" he asked.

"I heard you're three miles west of town?"

"That's it. It's got a 'Witten Ranch' sign over the gate. Be there before six tomorrow morning. What's your name, by the way?"

"Troy MacAlan... Mack to most."

Chapter Seven

"Let's tour the rest of town, Patch," I said, as I stepped out of Kristine's. We passed Myron's again, and I waved through the window.

We glanced in a number of stores, shops and offices, then reached the end of the boardwalk. A short ways ahead, I saw a fence surrounding a very nice gray, two-story home. Above the gate a sign read, "Ann Marie Undahl, M.D." Below that it said, "Family Doctor."

"Well, have a look at that Patch. The town doctor is a lady." I paused, then added, "Interesting." He glanced at me with a look that said, *Not that interesting*.

Across the street there was another very nice home, and it also had a sign. It read "Rev. James Thomas" across the top, and "Pastor, Eagle Bluff Christian Church" on the bottom. "Curious," I said, looking down at Patch, who hung on my every word, waiting for more enlightenment. "The parsonage on this end of town, the church on the other."

We climbed the steps onto the opposite boardwalk, and worked our way north until we reached the hotel door at the corner. I paused, considering a short nap, then remembered the gold in my saddlebag. "Guess we might as well tour the rest of town," I told Patch. "We can fetch the saddle bags while we're down that way."

At the east edge of town, we reached the Church and crossed over to Big Jake's. In his blacksmith shop, he was pumping the bellows to fire the coals in his forge. When he glanced up, I said, "Just stopped by to grab my saddlebags."

"Sure thing. They're still strapped to your saddle." He went to his tack room and untied the bags. "Here you go."

"What time are you here in the morning?" I asked.

"Usually by sun-up."

"I'll probably be here shortly after that to get Blaze. I'm starting work at the Witten ranch."

"Good for you. He's one of the best."

Bags in hand, I said, "See you in the mornin'."

Back at the hotel, I saw Pat. His back was turned, and it looked like he was putting mail in the slots. "How you doin', Pat?" I called out.

His head spun around. "Oh, hello, Mack. I'm doin' mighty fine. How can I help you?"

"I wanted to be sure that you're okay with Patch staying in the room with me. He's well-behaved, and quiet."

"Yes, I've noticed how well-behaved he is," he said, smiling at Patch. "That'll be just fine."

In the room, I laid my holster and saddle bags on a chair next to the bed within easy reach. "Why don't you lay down here next to the bed, and we'll take a short nap. Then we'll go have us some supper," I told Patch.

I'd been feeding him left-over scraps, but knew we needed something better as a steady diet. Roger Slenz, owner of the Eagle Bluff General Store, told me of a new "pellet" dog food that was much more healthy.

"Tomorrow, after working at the Witten ranch, we'll buy a bag of that food, Patch." He turned around in a circle, then curled up on the floor. *Not that concerned*, I thought.

I stretched out on the bed, my head nestled in a soft, silky pillow, and in no time at all I was in that wonderful unknown we call sleep. I slept hard for about forty-five minutes, when I was awakened by Patch's low growl. I rolled over, and saw he was still lying on the floor next to the bed. His head was stretched forward, and his eyes were glued to the door, as he continued with his low growl.

"Okay Patch. It's okay," I whispered.

He quickly glanced at me, then back at the door, eyes locked on what he had heard. I moved to the door, listened for a moment, then slowly turned the knob and eased the door open. I saw a guy trying to sneak away on his tip-toes, being as quiet as he could. He wore black boots, a black holster, and black hat. The hat had two bird feathers stuck in the right side of the hat band.

"So, whatcha up to, Tippy-Toes?" I whispered softly, as I eased the door shut. "We'll be watchin' for him, won't we buddy." Patch raised his ears in complete agreement.

In the corner of our room was a commode, with a pitcher of water and a basin. I poured water into the basin, splashed my face a few times, and grabbed the towel hanging on the side of the commode. I felt refreshed and, reaching for my gun belt, said, "Let's go out for some air, Patch."

Wondering what to do with the saddle bags, I shrugged and laid them at the foot of the bed, flopped the covers over them, and hoped it would look like just a bundle of blankets. I carefully adjusted it so I could tell if anyone had snooped around. "Okay Patch, let's go."

31

Passing the registration desk, I noticed Pat was not there. Instead, a very pleasant looking woman sat writing in a ledger. I paused, saying, "You don't look like the Pat Kennedy I know."

"Thank heaven for that," she said, and smirked.

Tipping my hat, I said, "I'm Mack... room 27."

"Hello, 'Mack Room 27.' That's a very interesting name." She showed a wry grin, as she nodded her head. "I'm Linda. I clerk for Pat several times a week, and help with his bookkeeping, too."

"Glad to meet you, Linda."

She looked at Patch. "Well, ain't you a handsome fella. And I'll bet as charming as you are handsome."

"That's Patch," I told her.

She crouched, saying, "Hello, Patch." He wiggled to get closer to her, and she began scratching behind his ears and under his chin. "So sweet, too."

I smiled as he looked up at me almost swooning. When she stood, I said, "We better let you get back to your work. Pleasure meeting you."

"Nice meeting the two of you," she responded, watching Patch follow me away.

When we passed the swinging doors to the saloon, there was a much higher level of activity than I'd heard before. I stepped in thinking I'd check things out, and had Patch lie beside the door out of the way of traffic. As I moved toward the bar, a short, wiry bartender headed my way.

"What can I get'cha?" he asked, with a friendly manner.

"I'll have a glass of beer."

"You got it."

He poured a mug full, and slid it in front of me. "That'll be a nickel."

I put a dime on the bar, and told him, "I'll probably be having another."

He tapped the dime with his finger, and let it lay. Then he pointed and nodded toward Patch. "Mighty fine looking dog you have there."

"Yup. That's Patch. He's a keeper."

It was a big saloon, with ten round tables, each surrounded by six chairs. Near the far wall was a silent upright piano. Two of the tables had poker games going on. One was full with six players, and the other had four playing. At the end, by the piano, were two Black Jack tables. One sat empty, and the other had two very serious players watching a dealer shuffle the deck. Along the bar, stood seven men joking and laughing.

One of the men left the group, and came my way. As he neared, he asked, "New in town?"

"Yup. New in town."

He swung his thumb over his left shoulder. "How 'bout you and I go over and join in that poker game. That'll make it six, and a good full game."

"I'm not much of a poker player," I told him. "You go right ahead."

He paused, gave me a stare, then said, "Well, then, how about you have a shot of whiskey with me."

My first thought was, *More whiskey is not what you need.* Instead, I said, "Thanks, but I'm not much for whiskey either."

He scoffed saying, "Not much for poker... not much for whiskey... what are you good for?"

"Probably not much... to you."

He glared at me, then growled, "Trying to mock me are ya, stranger?"

I started to say, "No, sir..." but saw his shoulder twitch, and his hand move toward his gun. I quickly stepped into him and, with my left arm, blocked him from drawing his gun. At the same time, I slammed my right hand hard into his throat, grabbed hold and squeezed. Bending him backward over the bar, I took the gun from his holster and slid it down the bar.

Still squeezing hard, I glared into his eyes saying, "Mister, I'm not looking for any kind of trouble, but you'd better be careful how you pick up that gun and holster it. Otherwise, you'll have more trouble than you ever wanted. Got that?"

Instead of answering, he struggled to free himself. I blocked him, pushed harder on his throat, and shouted louder, "Got that?"

34

He choked out an answer, whispering, "Okay... okay."

He was red-faced as he grabbed his gun, holstered it, then headed for the door. I watched his every move, until I saw him outside the window, climbing on his horse. I turned back to the bartender, saying, "Sorry to be causing you trouble."

"No need to be sorry. Charlie always figures he can bully his way around... marking his territory or something. Never seen him shoot anyone, but he figgers he can cower everybody by drawing down on 'em. You're one of the few that I've seen call his bluff."

I glanced over at Patch, who had been voicing a low growl the whole time. "It's okay, Patch."

Looking back at the barkeep, I said, "I try to stay away from trouble like that... whenever I can. Don't want to build a reputation as a troublemaker."

"You sure don't have to worry about that when you're dealing with the likes of Charlie," he replied.

"My name's Mack, by the way."

"Mine's Thaddeus James Quentin." He reached to shake my hand. "Call me Jimmy."

I finished my second beer, and set the mug on the bar. "I'm headed across the hall for some supper, Jimmy. See you again."

"Come back soon," he said, with a nod and a smile. "You're always welcome here."

35

Chapter Eight

Early the next morning, I rode to Will Witten's ranch. I got there at quarter of six and met Will, who introduced me to Stumpy Giles, his hired man. "Stumpy's been with me more than four years now. And, I'm sorry Mack, I don't remember your full name."

"Troy MacAlan. Mack's good enough."

"He doesn't remember my name either," Stumpy said.

"What is it?" I asked.

"Aldus Ambrose Giles," he proclaimed, grinning. "But if you call me by that, I might not even answer you. I can hardly remember it myself."

"Stumpy's a whole lot easier," I said, smiling back at him. He was about five-foot-four, with a strong, stocky build, and a little extra roll around his belt line. The nickname of Stumpy seemed to fit him just fine.

With the wagon loaded, he and I headed across the range to the south fence line. He explained how the Wittens were among the first of the ranchers in the area to fence their property's boundary lines. "This south fence line runs four miles east and west."

Rolling west, following the fence, he explained, "This first two-and-a-half miles was the border between us and the Johnston place. Now the Kennedys have taken over the place, and none of that fence was messed with. Five hundred feet down the line is where all the trouble starts.

"So, how does that happen?" I asked, sarcastically.

"Awful strange ain't it? They've tried to get Will to sell for more than a year. He won't, and lots of troublesome things keep happenin'. Up ahead you'll see how they cut up wire, broke off posts, and generally made a mess."

"Whoever it is doing this sure goes through a lot of work to cause some grief," I said.

"Yeah, and that ain't the worst of it. We had about two hundred head of cattle get loose. Took us three days to round 'em up, and we're still missin' a few."

"You think the Kennedys are behind it?"

"Yup. Think so. Will and Julie just don't have enemies, so it's the only thing that makes any sense. Maybe they figure that with enough trouble, he'll finally surrender and sell out. That's what happened with the Johnstons."

"What happened with them?"

"They had a long stream of things. A fire burned one of their sheds in the middle of the night, and nearly got to their barn. Fences were tore down, and some of their cattle rustled. What finally broke 'em, was when Mrs. Johnston's prize horse was shot in their south pasture. After that she insisted they sell and move on."

I shook my head. "Man, they play rough."

We went to work digging and setting new fence posts. There's lots of posts in a half-mile of fence line, so it was slow progress. With each one, we dug a three foot hole, set a seven foot post in it, then backfilled and packed the dirt with a heavy maul.

I paused, wiping sweat from my forehead and eyes with my bandana, then wiped the inside of my hat. I held the hat high to shade the hot, white, mid-day sun from my eyes. In the distance, I could see another fence line running through the Witten land. On the other side, was their large herd of cattle, lazily grazing. Then I noticed a rider in the distance, with two extra horses in tow.

"Must be Will," Stumpy said, squinting to see.

Soon, Will rode up with two saddled horses. "I decided to come and fetch you for dinner. Julie is cooking some pork chops, mashed potatoes and green peas. Think that's a whole lot better than me bringing you cold grub."

"Got that right," Stumpy told him with a smirk.

We mounted up, and loped back to the ranch house, with Patch running alongside. Stumpy and I stopped at the well to splash off the dust. After drying off, we headed into the house.

Will's wife, Julie, is very pleasant, and a great cook. The aroma that filled their home had my mouth watering. The pork chops she served were delicious.

I guess Stumpy thought so, too. After his first bite, he hummed, "Mmm, mmm, mmm!"

"Oh Stump, you're always trying to stay on my good side, no matter what I fix," she scoffed, as she wiped her hands on her apron.

"Oh no, it's not just flattery," he mumbled, still chewing. "These are the best pork chops... in the whole history of pork chops."

"Oh you," she said, slapping him on the shoulder.

She is petite, standing about five-foot-one, and maybe a hundred 'n ten pounds. Her red wavy hair was shoulder length, and tied back with a ribbon. I imagined when she went to town, or to a barn dance, or Sunday morning church, she might wear it brushed out and wavy. She was a handsome woman, with lightly freckled skin.

Stump had told me that she was a school teacher in Carson City when Will met her. Will's first look at her took his breath away, and for several months he rode to Carson City often. Finally, deciding this was way too much time spent on horseback, he asked her to marry him.

She said, "Yes!" and they were married in Eagle Bluff. That was two years ago, and Stumpy was one of many who were mighty glad Will had found Julie.

After a bit, my thoughts came back to the current problems. I said to Will, "Sounds like the Kennedys are likely behind the troubles you've had."

He considered it for a few moments, then shrugged and said, "Seems to be the only way it adds up. Each time I've told them I won't sell, they've gotten less friendly, and we've gotten more trouble."

"What does Sheriff Dawson have to say about it?"

"Not much he can say. We've never had a lick of proof. And... without proof...."

We ate our dinner, and rode back to the fence line. As we neared the wagon, I noticed a lone rider moving along the bottom of a ridge to the south. "See that rider?" I asked, still holding my focus on him.

Staring for a moment, Stumpy said, "Ya know, I've seen a rider on a white horse like that before. Always in the distance... always in the shadows."

"Hard to say who he is, or what he might be up to," Will said. He dropped us at the wagon, and headed back to the ranch house with the extra horses in tow. Stumpy and I went back to our digging, and setting posts. Patch laid in the shade of the wagon, sometimes napping, sometimes watching us, and sometimes glancing in the direction where the lone rider had been.

42

Chapter Nine

To pass the time as we worked, Stump and I talked about lots of things, getting to know one another a bit more. He told me, "Ya know, I live in the bunkhouse off the back of the barn, 'n there's plenty of room for you to move in. Better'n payin' for a hotel room."

"Sounds like a good idea," I said.

"It's a right nice, comfortable place, too."

At supper that evening, Stump told Will and Julie, "I suggested Mack move in the bunkhouse with me."

"Good idea," Will said. "If we run out of work for you, we might have to charge you a few nickels for rent and meals, but you're sure welcome to stay."

"Fair enough," I replied.

"And you won't have to be so lonesome out there, Stump," Julie joked.

"Yeah, I'm such a lonely guy," he pouted, feigning sadness.

"I'll stay in town tonight, and not likely be here 'till ten or so tomorrow," I told them. "I need to pick up some supplies, and take care of a few other things."

"That's fine," Will said. "I've got some things for Stump to do until you get here."

In town the next morning, I found a sack of dog food for Patch, and tied it behind the saddle. Then I stopped at Jeff's gun shop. I remembered he had some spyglasses, and I wanted to take a look at them. I stepped in and Jeff said, "Howdy Mack. What can I do for you?"

"I thought I'd check out your spyglasses."

"Well, I've got four different ones over here," he told me, as he led me to the shelf. "Whatcha got in mind?"

"I've always wanted one for hunting and such, so I thought I'd look for a good one."

"These are all good," he said, waving his hand over three of them. "They bring things in pretty clear, and aren't gonna break the bank. They're priced at five to six dollars each. But... this Pinkham & Smith, now that's a spyglass. It's a four draw that closes to twelve inches, and extends to thirty inches. It brings things in from long range, with sharp, clear detail."

"How much is it?"

"Fourteen dollars. But if you want a good one..."

"Let's go have a look," I said. Taking the Pinkham & Smith, and one of the other glasses, we stepped out to the boardwalk. I saw two women far down the street talking in front of the Doctor's house. Looking through the less expensive one, I could see them clearly.

Then I switched to the Pinkham & Smith and whispered, "Whoa!" I not only saw their features more clearly, I could see their eyelashes. I lowered the glass and looked it over. "You're right. I'll take this one."

As I left Jeff's, I thought about my bag of gold nuggets, and decided it was time to cash 'em in. I remembered seeing the Assay Office two doors down from the Sheriff. Nelson Mills, the agent, was impressed with my stash of gold. "How'd you come by such a good bit of high-grade ore?" he asked.

Without hesitating, and trying to look unconcerned, I said, "Me and a partner been panning for the past couple years, near Nevada City. I grew real tired of it, took my share, and left everything else to him. Figured it was time to bank the money."

Coming up with such a story on the spot surprised me... and also left a taste of guilt.

He weighed the gold, checked and double checked his figures, then said, "You have nine hundred and twenty-seven dollars' worth."

"Really," I said, trying hard not to show my surprise. "You wouldn't short-change me any... would ya?"

"No sir, I always give full value. Any place else you'd likely get less." He held the pouch toward me, and said, "You're welcome to check in other towns."

I said, "No, Nelson, you seem like an honest man. And you've gotta make a livin', too. It's a deal."

Next, I crossed the street and walked in the Nevada Territorial Bank. "I'd like to open an account," I told the teller.

"Mr. Bray will help you," he replied, pointing toward a man behind a desk.

Mr. Bray did help me, and I surprised him with the amount of my deposit. Finished with our business, I headed outside. I breathed in the fresh morning air, stretched and felt satisfied with having taken care of business.

Unwrapping the reins from the rail, I patted Blaze on the neck, and swung into the saddle. "C'mon Patch," I said, "we've got our chores done, let's head for the ranch."

He gave me a look that said, *It's about time, Mack. We've been patiently waiting all morning.*

Chapter Ten

When we got to the Witten ranch, Julie, Will and Stumpy had just finished branding some of their stock. "We had fifty-eight calves we hadn't branded," Will said. "Hate brandin' 'em, but it's necessary to mark what's ours."

Stumpy saw the puzzled look I had, as I gazed at their corral and chute set-up. "Unlike most, we brand 'em standin' up," he said. "We move 'em through the chute, and into the gates at the end. Then we put the iron on 'em as they're held in place.

"They get to squallin' their objections, but we open the gate quick, and they head out into the pasture on a dead run. They seem to be okay in no time."

"That's quite a system," I said, impressed with their ingenuity. "What's your brand?"

"JWW," Stumpy replied. "For Julie and Will Witten. Just added the 'J' when they got married."

As we got ready to head out for fence work, I laid my saddle bags in the wagon. "I've got food for Patch, and an extra canteen of water," I said, not mentioning my new spyglass that I wanted along in case we saw the lone rider in the area again.

We spent the morning digging holes and setting posts. Just before noon I saw Patch perk up, and turned to see Will riding toward us. "Looks like some eats comin' our direction," I told Stumpy.

He stuck his shovel in the ground saying, "Glad to hear it. I'm mighty dang hungry." He grabbed the makin's from his shirt pocket, and began rollin' a cigarette. He'd smoked since he was twelve, so building one was as second nature as strapping on his holster, or pulling on his boots. He held his tobacco pouch out toward me in an offering sort of gesture.

"No," I said, holding up a hand. "Never took it up. Thanks for the offer anyway."

"Good for you... I reckon," he said with a shrug. He struck a match, held the flame to the tip of the cigarette, and brought it to life.

Soon, Will rode up, shouting, "Noon-time delivery." He had two sandwiches for each of us. We sat on the ground, leaning against the wagon wheels, and taking advantage of what little shade the wagon gave. My first bite reminded me of just how hungry I was. I eased into a conversation about the Kennedys, again, asking Will, "What do you think their purpose is, buying up ranches like they are?"

"Well..." he hesitated as he swallowed, "the only thing I can figure, besides them trying to have the biggest ranch in the area, is gaining control of Rush Creek. The father, Brendan Kennedy, has six thousand acres about seven miles west. Adam owns five thousand acres five miles southeast of here. Rush Creek runs through Brendan's ranch, our ranch, then on down to Adam's. Now they have the Johnston's and the two spreads between me and Brendan."

I took another bite of my sandwich, while I considered what he'd said. After a drink from my canteen, I asked, "What about his other son, Sean, the one that owns the newspaper, where does he live?"

48

"He's always lived in town, but now I hear he's the one trying to buy the ranch on the other side of Brendan. That would give them control of nearly twenty miles of Rush Creek, with our ranch as the only gap."

I nodded. "I can see why they want yours, then. But, I don't see it as cause for the kind of trouble that's been happenin'."

"Yeah, 'n I just heard the worst of it," he said, as he looked over toward Stumpy. "You know Rocky Wilson, the rancher west of Brendan's place that's been missing for the past week... well Sheriff Dawson stopped by this morning to tell us they found his body yesterday. It was in the brush at the base of the hills along the south edge of his land. He said Rocky had taken two bullets in the chest, and then was drug into the brush."

Stumpy shook his head, sadly. "Damnation... things just keep gettin' nastier, and more hateful. I'd like to get a bead on the varmint that's behind all this."

Will swallowed his last bite of sandwich, then drank from his canteen. After staring out at the horizon for a time, he said, "I'm sure Mrs. Wilson will sell now."

For a while we were all quiet. Like me, they were likely thinking about the notion of a man being shot over the buying and selling of his land. Hearing Patch stir under the wagon, I turned, and saw him staring south.

I stood and leaned on the side of the wagon, trying to pick out what he'd seen. Finally, I noticed movement at the bottom of a distant ridge. It looked like it could be that same lone rider on the white horse.

By now Will and Stumpy had stood, and were looking too. "What do you see?" Will asked.

"See that highest crop of rocks on that ridge," I said, pointing. "Look down and to the right a little. I think it's that lone rider."

I brought out my spyglass, extended it, then heard Stumpy say, "Well, look at that, would ya," as he bumped Will's arm with the back of his hand. "Got himself a pretty nice piece there."

I raised the glass to my eye, and focused on the rider. "It's a white horse all right, with a black saddle," I told them. The rider was wearing a gray Stetson that shaded his face. He continued to move our direction, unaware that we were watching. Soon I could see that the right side of his face had heavy burn scars. Then he stopped, and turned in his saddle to look behind him. As he did, I saw the left side of his face was even more scarred.

"His face has some serious burn scars," I told them, as I lowered the glass. Then, touching my cheek, I added, "The right side is scarred, but the left side...." I rubbed my hand all over the left side of my face. "The left is one big scar. Looks like a piece of wrinkled, reddish-brown leather covering that whole side."

Reaching out with the glass, I said, "Have a look, Will. See if you recognize anything about him. Maybe you've seen him in the area before."

He focused, studied for a few moments, then slowly lowered the glass. "Nope, I don't recognize him or his horse. See what you think, Stump," he said, handing the glass to Stumpy.

He had the same reaction, adding, "He looks to be just a bit on the fearsome side. Wouldn't care to meet up with him in a boxed canyon."

I reached for the glass as Stumpy held it out, then I took one more look. As I lowered and closed it, I said, "I'd like to ride out there and have a talk with him, but I'm sure he'd disappear before I got halfway. And there's not much sense spending the rest of the day tracking him"

"No, not worth it," Will agreed. "I'll start asking around, see if anyone knows anything of him."

"It's a little strange, the way he lurks in the area like he does," I said, as I put the glass away.

Through the coming days we finished replacing the half mile of fence. The last afternoon, as we sat on the back of the wagon having a cool drink of water from our canteens, Stumpy said, "I think Will's got some work for us back at the ranch. He wants to add a new corral on the south side of the barn. After that, we'll run a check on the rest of the fence lines, and repair whatever needs it."

That evening at supper, I said to Will, "I'd like to spend a day in town, do a little nosing around to see what I can find out about the Kennedys buying up ranches along Rush Creek. Maybe something about who's behind all the trouble. And... anything about our friend Scarface hanging around in the shadows."

He lowered his coffee cup. "Tomorrow would be a good day for that. Stump and I have some things to finish up, then Friday we can go to work on the new corral. Likely have it finished by Saturday evening, and can relax on Sunday."

51

Julie offered a piece of cake, and I held up my thumb and forefinger. "Just a small piece, please."

"Okay, if you insist," she said, cutting one in half.

"I'm too full," I groaned, rubbing my stomach. "But it looks so, so good, I can't pass on it." Taking the first bite, I hummed, "Mmm, mmm, mmm."

"You're starting to sound like him now," she drawled, pointing to Stumpy. He sat there with a big grin.

"Oh no, it's the honest truth. I never lie with Patch listening," I said, as I glanced toward where he lay. His head lifted, and he gave me a look of, *why am I being roped into this?*

Will asked, "What are you hoping to find in town? Don't know if there's anything to be found."

"There's got to be a thread running through this. Something that ties it all together... makes some sense of it. Maybe with some nosing around, new eyes looking, a little luck... who knows?"

"It'll be well worth the time if you can make any sense of it all," Julie said, slowly shaking her head, showing her frustration.

"I'll probably head into town after breakfast, and may not be back until late tomorrow night."

"Just be sure to take off your boots 'n sneak in real quiet like when you get back," Stumpy growled, with a stern look. Then he flashed his big, wide grin.

Chapter Eleven

In town the next day, I stopped at the barber shop to ask Myron if he had time for dinner at Kristine's. "My treat," I told him, which brought a cheerful agreement.

As we left his shop, he sorted through several signs that stood behind his door. He pulled one out that read, "I'm at Kristine's," hung it on the door, and pulled it closed behind us. In Kristine's, Myron introduced me to Karlee Kay, the waitress who brought us coffee.

Myron blew on the hot coffee, then asked, "I heard you're workin' for Will Witten. How's that goin'?"

"Just fine," I told him, then sipped my coffee. "Will and Julie are terrific folks."

"Two of the best," he agreed. "How 'bout Stumpy?"

"He's a real hoot... and a hard worker."

Karlee Kay came back to take our orders. She was tall and attractive, and seemed very sweet. I asked, "What's really good today?"

"I think the meatloaf and mashed potato dinner is the best today," she said, with a wide, pretty smile.

"That's what I'll have, then."

"Would you like corn or green peas with that?" she asked, as she wrote the order.

"I'll go with the corn."

Still writing, she asked, "And you Myron?"

"I'll have the same, only with green peas. And more coffee, when you have a minute."

"Right back with it," she said, heading for the kitchen.

After some small talk, I asked Myron, "I know you're not fond of the Kennedys, but what do you think about them buying up all the ranches along Rush Creek?"

"There's been a heap of opinion and rumor about that for more'n a year," he said. "Some figure they want the biggest ranch in the territory. Rush Creek running through it all would eliminate any worry about water.

"Then there's been rumors of gold along Rush Creek. Lots of speculatin'," he scoffed, with a broad wave of his blue-veined hand, as though dismissing the notion.

"What about all the trouble for the past year, and I just heard about the murder of Rocky Wilson."

"Well... yes... that's a puzzler. Everything seems to point toward the Kennedys, and most folks put the blame on them." He said it as though he didn't agree with most.

I waited, as he considered it more.

He looked up from his coffee cup. "As much as I've disliked their ways, I just don't see them doing those kinds of things. 'Specially the killing. But, who knows?"

Karlee Kay came with our dinners, so I thought I'd lighten the conversation as we began eating. "Where did you start barbering, Myron?"

"Kansas City. I grew up there, learned barbering there, and married Catherine there," he said, with a sad smile. "I barbered there for forty years, and was married to my Catherine for forty-one years." It was a very proud statement, laced with sadness.

Looking at him, I was still amazed that he was seventy years old. Had I not known, I'd have guessed him to be just turning sixty. I asked, "What happened?"

"I lost her in the influenza epidemic. After that I heard from a friend who'd passed through this area, that Eagle Bluff didn't have a barber. So, I decided it would be good to make a fresh start. That was ten years ago."

"Still have family in Kansas City?"

"No, not really. We couldn't have children, and most of our families have passed on. Only one or two left that I write to. How 'bout you, Mack? Any family?"

I hesitated, not sure. Something always lingered just on the edges, so I wasn't sure of my past. It was just me, here and now.

"No," I said. "No family. I'm from over Wyoming way. Never married, though I almost did once. My folks and my brother have passed on. So, it's just me." *Getting good at spinning yarns on the spot*, I thought... feeling a pang of guilt again.

Chapter Twelve

Staring out the window, I noticed a guy working in the street with a pitchfork and shovel. He was busy pitching manure into a horse-drawn wagon. Curious, I asked, "Who's that fella, Myron?"

He glanced, then said, "Oh, that's our Kenny Page. He keeps the street clean." He saw how puzzled I looked, and continued. "It's a long, long story that started twenty years ago. Back then, when Kenny walked into Eagle Bluff, he was fifteen years old. He'd been orphaned since he was nine, and everyone wondered how he had made it through life for that long on his own. You see, Kenny is a little slow... likely some sort of brain disorder. He speaks slowly, and behaves a mite differently.

"Well, Paul Udahl, who runs the Post Office and the Overland Stagecoach office, took him under his wing. They have a room in the back of their office, so Paul moved a bunk in there, figuring Kenny could stay for a few days. Kenny's lived there ever since.

"Later, that first day, Kenny asked Paul if he had a shovel and a pitchfork. Naturally, Paul wondered about it, and asked, 'What do you need it for, Kenny?'

"'Manure all over the street... big mess,' he said quietly, staring and pointing toward the street.

"Paul figured it couldn't hurt anything, and would keep Kenny occupied for a while. He fetched the tools for him, and Kenny went to work shoveling manure into piles along the boardwalk.

57

"Soon, the Sheriff noticed him outside his window and, curious, stepped out to see who it was, and what he was up to. He watched for a few moments, then said, 'Hello there, son. What'cha doin'?'

"Kenny stopped, stood staring down at the street, then softly said, 'Shoveling.'

"'Oh, I see. Whose shovel do you have?'

"'Paul's shovel,' he answered, pointing toward the Post Office, while still staring down at the street. He seldom raised his eyes.

A soft smile creased the sheriff's lips. "'What's your name, son?'

"'Kenny Page.'

"'Hello Kenny, my name is Stoney. Stoney Dawson. You go right on with your work. You're doing a fine job there, and I don't want to get in your way.'"

Myron drank some of his coffee, then continued. "As Kenny went back to his shoveling, Stoney walked over to see Paul. After discussing it, the Sheriff said, 'As long as he's workin' that hard, I'm gonna find a wagon for him, and a horse to pull it. He can haul the manure to that deep ravine just east of town.'"

Myron set his cup down. "You see, whatever brain disorder Kenney has, it results in him fixatin' on certain things. His primary fixation, for the past twenty years, has been keeping Main Street clean. Stoney got the town council to hire him. They pay him enough to afford rent for his room, groceries, and a few nickels for spending money.

"So... that's our Kenny. Everyone looks after him, and will give him little jobs as they can."

I watched Kenny through the window, and felt a smile forming. After a bit, I looked back at Myron. "That's a wonderful thing you folks have done."

"It is," he responded. "But Kenny does a fine thing for us, too. And I'm not talking about keeping the street clean... he keeps us humble."

I nodded, letting silence say the rest.

We finished eating, and Myron drank down the last of his coffee. "I'd better be gettin' back to the shop," he said. "I saw Herman Schmidt wave in the window a while ago, so he's probably waiting in my chair."

I stood, reached out my hand, and said, "Thanks for joining me, Myron."

"Any time, Mack. Thanks for dinner... and for your good company."

Chapter Thirteen

Outside, I thought I'd dig into the notion of gold on Kennedy land. I brought out the bit of meatloaf I'd saved for Patch, and his tail thumped on the boardwalk. "How 'bout a treat?" I said. He took it gently from my hand, devoured it in two quick chomps, then looked up, hoping for more.

"I'm gonna go visit George at the Assay Office," I told him. "You wait here."

George did a double-take when I stepped in. "Hello, Mack. Back with more gold?"

"No," I said, laughing. "Here for some knowledge."

"Well, I've got little to offer," he joked.

I explained about working for the Wittens, and trying to check into problems they've had. "Have you had any gold come in from along Rush Creek in the past year?"

He stared past me, giving it some thought, then said, "None I recall. But there was a time, about a year and a half ago, that Conner Kennedy brought some to be assayed. Said it was from the Carson River, but I'd never seen gold come from the area he referred to. I kind of wondered about that.

"There's a Conner Kennedy, too?" I asked, more than a little surprised.

"Yes. I think he was the third oldest brother. Adam, Patrick, then Conner, and then Sean. Anyway, nothing more came of that bit of gold before he went to prison."

61

"He's in prison?" I choked out, surprised again.

"Well no, not any more anyway. He was killed, while in prison, almost a year ago."

"What?" was all I could say. My mind was spinning, trying to piece it together.

"Yup and, since then, Brendan Kennedy has been taking all of his land business over to Carson City. I figured he did it for privacy. And if he's had any gold dealings it would be with Bill Nelson, the agent over there in Carson City. You might check with him about any gold findings."

"Sounds like it might be worth the ride," I said, considering all this new information. "Maybe get lucky, and find more pieces to this puzzle."

Back on the boardwalk, Patch dutifully guarded Blaze from all of life's perils. When he saw me, he sat up, panting excitedly. I scruffed his neck, saying, "You're such a good dog, Patch," and his whole body wagged with joy. "You'll have to stay here and guard Blaze a little longer. I'm gonna walk over to see if the Sheriff is in."

I walked to his office, just two doors down, and I glanced back at Patch as I got there. He lay on the boardwalk, head up, ears alert, dutifully on guard.

"Good boy, Patch," I said, and his tail began swishing back and forth on the boardwalk. Opening the door to the Sheriff's office, I called out, "Hello?"

The Sheriff, who was in the back, where I assumed the jail cells were located, shouted, "Hello," then came around the corner.

I stood at the wood rail that separated the waiting area from the Sheriff's desk. Behind the Sheriff's desk was a beautiful gun rack that held eight or ten rifles and shotguns. To the left of his desk, near the wall, was a potbelly stove that stood cold for the summer. As he rounded the corner, he asked, "Can I help you?"

"Hello, Sheriff. I'm Troy MacAlan." I stepped through the swinging gate, and extended my hand.

He shook it, saying, "Hello, Mr. MacAlan. Nice to finally meet you. I've heard good things."

"Call me Mack," I said.

He nodded his agreement, and said, "Call me Stoney."

He was my height, and had a husky build. His thinning hair was white and clipped short, and he sported a white, handlebar mustache. I guessed him to be in his early fifties.

"I heard you started working for Will Witten a short while ago," he said. "I also heard, from Jimmy at the Eagle Bluff Saloon, how you handled Charlie without letting it get out of control."

"Well, I did what seemed right at the moment," I said, feeling a little flush in my face.

"I wish there were more like you. I've been at this sheriffing business for over thirty years now, and I'm looking for a good deputy that can take over in the coming year." He paused, pulling out his desk chair and sitting down. As he pointed to a chair for me, he added, "Maybe you'd be interested in the job?"

63

I hesitated, then finally said, "I'm flattered... but not knowing how long I'll be in Eagle Bluff, I'll have to give you a no for the time being."

"Fair enough. But if you do decide to stay, I hope you'll consider my offer. You're the kind we need to fill this job. Maybe lift it up another level." He leaned back in his chair, then asked, "So, how can I help you?"

"I'm doing a little nosin' into the stuff that's been happening as the Kennedys have been buying up ranches. I might be steppin' in your business a bit, but I figure there's a thread running through all this that would tie it together."

"I agree. And you don't have to worry a bit about steppin' on any toes. I'm always glad for any help, no matter where it comes from."

"I got three things stuck in my craw," I said, "and I hoped you might know something about 'em. First, there's a lone rider with a heavily scarred face that lingers in the shadows. We've seen him a couple of times, and no one seems to know a thing about him."

"Yeah... I've heard that too. But I have no idea who he is, where he's from, or what he's up to."

"Okay. Second thing is the possibility of gold on the Kennedy land, or anywhere else along Rush Creek."

"Can't help with that either. I've heard rumors, but don't know if there's anything to it."

"Alright then, this last thing I just found out from George over at the assay office... Conner Kennedy being sent to prison, then killed there."

"That one I could talk your ear off about."

"Well, how 'bout the short version, for now."

"Even the short version will take a little while," he answered. "From a very young age, Conner was a handful," the Sheriff started. "Not just misbehaving, like most kids will do... not just stubbornness, like many... this kid was nasty, defiant and cruel in unimaginable ways. He gave Brendan and Kate, his parents, a lifetime of grief. The other three boys, who were a big handful on their own, looked mellow by comparison.

"I had run-ins with Conner regularly, especially in his teen years. Locked him up a few times. By the time he was nineteen, he was nearly shunned by his family. Then he was found guilty of murder, and sent to Nevada State Prison in Carson City."

"Sounds pretty rough," I said.

"He was really rough. Most of his nineteen years were a living hell for his family. And once they'd locked him up, I don't know if the family ever visited him in prison. A short while later, he was cut up pretty bad by another inmate, and didn't make it through."

I wondered about it all, then asked, "What's Brendan's background? How did he gather such wealth?"

"He's from Ireland, and married Kate over there. In 1854, they came to Carson City, hoping to get a piece of the gold mining action. Word of riches from the '49 rush had spread world-wide, and lots of immigrants began moving to the area hoping to get rich. Brendan and his partner found a small placer, and did pretty well for themselves."

65

"What's a placer?"

"Well, they're pockets of gravel that hold high grade ore. In '49, when all this started, two large placers were found — one off the Yuba River, the other near Deer Creek.

"Digging and panning soon gave way to sluice boxes. Then, eventually, hydraulic mining took it over. Then the big mining companies bought up most of it.

"Anyway, Brendan and his partner were doing pretty well, and that's when he bought his ranch. Later he set up his sons with businesses and ranches. I think he sold his gold business about a year and a half ago, then started buying more ranch land."

He paused, staring out the window, deep in thought. Looking back at me, he added, "And... that's when all the trouble started."

Chapter Fourteen

I thanked the sheriff, left his office, and walked back to where Patch and Blaze waited. When I sat on the edge of the boardwalk, Patch wiggled closer to me so I could scratch and pet him. I looked at Blaze, and said, "I think we'll need to take a ride to Carson City in the coming days. You up for that, girl?" She knickered softly, as though not sure of the idea, and Patch nudged me for more petting.

"We may have to make a visit Brendan Kennedy, too. Have a face-to-face chat with him." Patch lowered his head and rested on his outstretched paws, content with my plan.

It was still a while until suppertime, and I wasn't feeling hungry, so I thought we'd visit Dave at the Gazette office. Hopefully he could add to the Kennedy saga. I let Blaze drink her fill at a nearby trough, then swung into the saddle. "Let's go, Patch."

As we turned the corner, I noticed Charlie – the fella I'd had the run-in with at the saloon – strolling up the boardwalk. Likely headed to the Eagle Bluff Saloon, he was staring down as he walked, and didn't notice us. I saw the fur on Patch's back stand up, and said softly, "It's okay, Patch." He relaxed, glancing up at me to be sure everything was okay.

Just then, the swinging doors at the Dusty Eagle flew open, slamming against the wall. A long-haired, rough looking hombre was dragging a smaller, frightened looking guy out the door. The slight one flew from the boardwalk, landing face down in the dirt street with a thud. He lay there not moving... maybe not wanting to move.

The other jumped down from the boardwalk, shouting, "Get up you little weasel." I could tell he was steamed, but wondered about the big size advantage he had.

Maybe someone needs to step in, before the smaller one gets seriously hurt, I thought. I nudged Blaze forward, slowly moving closer to the ruckus. As I was ready to slide from the saddle, the bigger one shouted again.

"Get on your feet, you belly crawlin' coward." As he shouted, he kicked the smaller man's boot. Then he tore his hat from his head, and flung it at the man still cowering on the ground.

For a moment, I looked at the man lying in the dirt. Then, glancing back at the bigger man, I almost choked as I whispered, "What the...." I couldn't believe what I saw. I'm sure my mouth hung wide open, as I stared at the woman hovering over the man on the ground.

Before I could puzzle over it any further, a man came out the swinging doors of the saloon carrying a shotgun. The guy, who I found out later was Dusty, the saloon owner, shouted, "Rita, back away, and leave him alone."

Either she didn't hear him in the midst of her fury, or the noise of the gathering crowd was drowning out what he said. Either way, she paid no attention. Instead, she started to kick at the man again.

Dusty fired his shotgun in the air, which did get her attention. She spun around, her hand on her gun. In the same moment, I heard a shout from behind me. "Rita, take yer hand off that gun." I turned to see Sheriff Dawson storming up the street, looking madder'n blazes.

She took her hand from the gun, then faked like she was going to kick the small man one more time. "Rita!" the Sheriff growled again. "Just what in hell fire you tryin' to do here?"

She glared down at the small man on the ground saying, "Carson here, was runnin' his mouth about Doc Undahl, as if she'd even look twice at him. She's the finest lady in our town, and he just kept rattling on with his foul mouth. Guess I just blew up."

"Well, I guess you did just that," he growled. Then, staring at the man on the ground for a moment, and shaking his head, he barked, "Carson, get to your feet, and drag your sorry butt home.

"And you, Rita, pick up your hat, get on your horse, and point her toward home... before I arrest you for assault."

When I slid down from Blaze, the sheriff showed a small grin, and said, "Thanks Mack."

"For what?" I asked quietly.

"I could see, as I came up the street, you were gonna move in to try and calm things."

I shrugged, asking, "Who is she?"

He smiled again, looking past me to see Rita turn her horse toward home. Then he said, "She's Rita Mae Scott, better known as Ragin' Rita. Deadwood, South Dakota has their Martha Jane Burke... Calamity Jane. We've got our Ragin' Rita. She's no less fearsome a woman. Got the name for the way she goes off in a rage when she doesn't like something."

"You're right about that. She does look full of fire."

"And don't ever doubt it. You saw her for yourself. She's a little over six feet tall, and two hundred pounds. She's stronger than half the men I know, and never backs down from anything or anyone. She can handle herself... and her gun, too."

"Man-o-man!" I said, almost whispering.

"Man-o-man is right. She's a handful."

I glanced in the direction she'd gone, then said, "Well, I was on my way to see Dave over at the Gazette. So, now that the dust has settled..."

"Thanks again, Mack. Tell Dave howdy."

I walked in the newspaper office, and found Dave busy at his press. He shouted, "Hello, Mack. Come on in." Soon, the big plates slowed to a stop, and he grabbed a rag to wipe his hands.

"Hi there. You didn't have to shut it down."

"No problem. I'm just running a couple of proofs through to check 'em." Then he added, "You made the news this week."

"Really!" I said, surprised.

He grabbed one of the sheets from his press, laid it on his table, then pointed to a headline. It read, "Witten's Have New Hired Hand. Stumpy Has New Roommate." This was followed by a long paragraph describing the newcomer in town.

70

"How 'bout that. And look here," I said, reading further. "Even Patch made the news."

"Yup. Can't forget the faithful companion."

"Dave, I wondered what you could tell me about the Kennedys buying up ranches, or about Conner Kennedy."

"Not much about the Kennedys that you haven't already heard. And we did just the minimum on Conner's trial... and on his stabbing in prison."

"Who had he murdered?"

"It was Walt Jacoby, the hired man out at the Hayes Ranch. That's the place just east of Brendan Kennedy that they now own. Conner was supposedly trying to run Walt off Kennedy land, and ended up shooting him. Conner claimed that Walt drew on him. Trouble was, Walt lay dead on the Hayes' land. Conner's history in town— and even his own family's testimony – hurt him more than it helped."

"Things just seem to get more confounding," I said, scratching the back of my neck. I thanked him, adding, "Oh... and thanks for making us famous."

Chapter Fifteen

Out on the boardwalk, I could see that there was a bunch of horses tied in front of the hotel. "Let's leave Blaze here, Patch, instead of tying her in that crowd down there." As we neared, I saw Pat Kennedy in front of the hotel. It seemed he was finishing a conversation as we approached. Then he glanced my way, and said, "Hello, Mack."

"Howdy, Pat. Got time for supper?"

"I was just thinkin' about getting something to eat. Be glad to join you."

As we entered the Diner, I had Patch lie beside the doorway. Pat waved, saying, "Let's sit at my usual table." Then, looking back at patch, he added, "That's quite a dog you have there."

"He surely is," I agreed.

After the waitress took our order, he asked, "So, how are things going out at the Witten's?"

"Goin' fine. They're good people to work with."

He lowered his eyes. "I'm sure you've heard about some of the nasty trouble that's been happening, and that some of it is being blamed on my family."

Don't lie with Patch listening. "Yes, actually I've heard about it from several sources. Then again, I've also heard that some folks aren't so quick to condemn your family for what's been happening."

"Well, that's encouraging. We haven't been tried and convicted yet."

"No, not that I've heard. But it's such a coincidence of bad things happening to ranchers, until they finally decide to sell out to your family. So you can't blame folks for wondering."

"Yes, I know. Our difficulty is trying to prove innocence. A very difficult thing to do, particularly when we're less than beloved to begin with."

"I'd like to meet your father sometime. Do you think he'd be willing to meet with me?"

"I know he would. Despite what others may say, he's a very reasonable man."

"That's good," I said. "If you happen to talk with him, let him know for me."

Supper was delivered, interrupting our conversation. I hadn't had a steak in a while, so I'd ordered a T-bone. It was thick, juicy and delicious. I knew I wouldn't eat the whole thing, so I saved a chunk for Patch. As we were finishing, Pat asked if I'd like dessert.

"Can't finish this delicious steak... think I'll pass."

He ordered a slice of pie and, while we waited, I asked, "What can you tell me about... or, maybe I should ask, what are you willing to tell me about your brother Conner?"

"There's not a whole lot to tell beyond what's public knowledge. He was a holy terror growing up, and caused my folks endless grief."

74

"How did he die?"

"I guess he crossed the wrong guy in the state pen, one too many times. It was a guy you don't cross, and he carved Conner up pretty bad."

I shook my head. "Nasty stuff."

As we got ready to leave, Pat said, "I enjoyed your company. This one's on me."

"Thanks, but you don't have to do that."

"I know, but I want to. You've been good company, and it's been great to hear that not everyone blames us for all that's been happening."

As I left the restaurant, I glanced in the Saloon, then stopped and backed up. I looked in again, and saw black boots, black holster, black hat with two feathers. "Well, Tippy Toes," I whispered, then looked down at my sidekick. "Let's stop for a beer, Patch." Like before, he laid beside the door, and I walked to the end of the bar.

As the barkeep headed toward me, I said, "Hey, Jimmy, how's it goin'?"

"Goin' good, Mack. Get'cha a beer?"

"You got it."

While I visited with Jimmy, enjoying the beer, I kept an eye on the man in black, and his crowd. Soon their conversation got more animated, and I heard one of 'em point, saying, "That's him, alright."

I turned to Jimmy. "Who's the guy in the black hat?"

"Hal Dorski... ranch foreman for Adam Kennedy. You wanna watch out, he can be nasty."

"Thanks," I said. Then I heard footsteps coming my way, and glanced to see Tippy-Toes stepping up. I turned to face him, as he snarled, "So, you're the one that worked Charlie over." When he said it, he gave me a hard poke in the chest.

Chapter Sixteen

I stared at Dorski for a long moment, then told him, "I didn't work Charlie over at all. I stopped him from pulling his gun on me, and maybe shooting me. And... I don't make a habit of poking people in the chest, so I won't have anyone poking me in the chest."

"Is that right?" he barked, as his finger came at my chest again. I quickly grabbed his wrist, my thumb against the back of his hand. I bent it, and rolled it over, until both his wrist and his elbow were screaming at his brain. Then I pushed him away from me.

Rubbing his wrist and elbow, he said, "Think you're pretty tough, huh?" When he got the last syllable out, I saw his eyes twitch, and his shoulder begin to roll. When his fist came at me, I slapped at it, deflecting the punch from hitting its target. At the same time, I hit him hard in the chest with the heel of my open hand. It drove him back, gasping and clutching at his chest.

In a flash, determined to get the best of me, he went for his gun. I quickly stepped into him, rammed my arm between his hand and his holster, preventing him from drawing his gun, then stomped on his foot with my boot heel.

As he flinched, I shouted in his face, "Wait a minute!" It was loud enough to surprise him, even startle him.

"Wait a minute?" he asked. "Wait a minute?" he repeated with a puzzled look.

"Yes, wait a minute," I said, holding my hand up in a "stop" kind of motion. "Just hold on, and hear me out."

He stared in disbelief, and I continued. "Before we go for guns... again... let's go outside and try a little experiment. Then if you still want to go for your gun, have at it." I kept an eye on him as I moved toward the door, waving for him to follow. Patch had leaped to his feet, voicing his low growl. As I neared him, I said, "It's okay boy. Lay down."

Behind me, trying to regain his bravado in front of his followers, Hal shrugged, saying, "Okay boys, let's go see what kind of silly game he's got in mind."

Outside, I quickly checked my gun, as I stepped down from the boardwalk. When Hal followed, I said, "The rest of you folks stay on the boardwalk, out of the way of some shooting." I turned back to Hal. "Sometimes, if a man makes a decision without enough good information, he could make a terribly bad decision. Would you agree with me on that?"

"I'll give ya that," he crowed, wondering where this was headed.

"We're each gonna take a turn drawing and shooting at a target. Show what we can do with a gun... how fast and how good-a shot we are. With that new information, both of us can make a better decision about going for our guns against one another in the future."

He stared at me a long moment. Then, trying again to get the upper hand, he turned to the crowd, shook his head and pointed at me. "I think he's serious."

"I am serious."

This caught him up short. Finally he shrugged, and said, "Let's go then."

Glancing across the way, I saw that the sign over "Richard's Pharmacy and Eyeglasses" had a wooden arch atop it. Five wooden stars, each about the size of a man's hand, were spread across the top of the arch. I pointed, saying, "See those five stars on top of Richard's sign?"

"Yup," he drawled.

"Our targets. I'll repair his sign when we're through."

"Go right ahead," he proclaimed, to the laughs of his boys. "Show us your stuff."

"I'll start with the one on the far right. You can take the next one." I looked at the target, drew and fired. The star shattered, and flew from the sign. After the murmurs quieted, I said, "Your turn."

He looked at me, then looked up at the star. He wiggled his hand as though relaxing it, then drew his gun and fired. He hit the sign just below, and a few inches left of the star. He gave me a snarling, sideways look when I said, "Not bad."

"Just so there won't be any question about good luck or bad luck, let's try again." Without hesitation, I drew and fired, blowing away the second star. His look told me he knew how fast I was.

"You're up," I said.

He drew and fired, this time tearing a chunk from the edge of the sign, just below the star. "Not bad," I said, then drew and fired three quick shots, shattering the last three stars. I had loaded a cartridge in the empty sixth chamber of my gun on the way out, so I had one left... just in case.

"Now we both have a lot more information, and can make a better decision when it comes to pulling guns on one another," I said, looking him in the eye. Then I dropped my Colt in its holster.

Charlie, who worked for Hal, had come from the Dusty Eagle Saloon when he heard the ruckus. What he shouted to was, "Let's go have a beer, Hal." What the crowd heard in the way he said it was, "Don't be a fool, Hal."

"You know," I said, "I kind of got off on the wrong foot with you and Charlie. How 'bout I buy you boys a beer, and we let bygones be bygones."

Before anyone could say anything more, Jimmy shouted, "C'mon boys, let's all go have one." He gave a big wave, and everyone followed him back into the bar.

I was last in, and stopped to pet Patch, who dutifully remained in his place. I stroked his neck and shoulder, telling him, "I'm gonna have one more beer, then we'll head for the ranch." Then I said to Jimmy, "This round is on me. Set 'em up for everybody."

When he was done pouring drinks, he walked to the end of the bar with my beer, and a big grin. He asked, softly, "What in tar-nation inspired that?"

"Well, I knew how I stacked up against Hal. I just wanted to make sure that **he** understood. I didn't want him to do anything foolish. I hate the thought of shooting someone... anyone... no matter who it is."

Chapter Seventeen

At the ranch, Will, Stumpy and I spent the next two days building a new corral behind the barn. I told Will that I planned to ride over to Carson City. "George, the assay agent, said that Brendan Kennedy has taken his land dealings over there for the last year and a half. He figures if there's been any gold, he's taken that over there, too. I thought I'd leave tomorrow after breakfast, and be back late Tuesday afternoon."

Sunday morning, Julie gave me ham sandwiches. "These should hold you for the trip going," she said. "And here," she added, tossing me an apple. "Take this with you, too."

"Thanks a bunch. If I don't feel hungry for the apple, Blaze sure will."

She threw another. "Both of you enjoy one."

"Thanks, again," I said, waving as I stepped out the door. At the well, I rinsed my canteen and filled it with fresh, cool water. I had packed some food for Patch, so we were ready to travel.

We headed south for a couple miles, then picked up the trail west to Carson City. I figured we'd make it nearly three-fourths of the way, then camp somewhere along the trail. We'd been riding for a few hours, when I noticed a dust cloud against the horizon. It appeared slow-moving, but, as it got closer, it seemed to move faster and faster. Finally, with it not more than a half-mile away, I could see it was a stagecoach.

I steered Blaze toward a meadow to get wide of the dust cloud that would come our way. As the coach rolled closer, I read "Overland Stagecoach" painted on its side. It moved by at a pretty good pace, with the team of four horses holding a steady lope, and a sweaty sheen. I waved to the driver.

He waved back to us, shouting, "Howdy." Then he shifted in the box to get more comfortable, and gave his team a light slap with the reins.

Down the grassy slope, there was water flowing in a small creek. I walked Blaze to it, slid from the saddle, then took off her bridle and let her step in to drink. Patch joined her, lapping up the fresh water thirstily. I stretched, trying to loosen my tight muscles from sitting the saddle, then I stepped out on a flat rock, and bent to splash my face.

When they'd drank enough, I put my hand under Blaze's chin, and led her to the grassy slope for a little grazing. After putting two handfuls of dog food on the grass for Patch, I grabbed my canteen and grub, then stretched out on the ground. The soft, green slope was a nice oasis in this Nevada sagebrush territory.

Soon we were back on the trail headed west for Carson City. We stopped again in mid-afternoon for water, some food, and another short rest. As evening approached, the warm sun was casting a fiery, reddish-gold sunset. The buttes and mountains looked aglow, shining reddish-brown above the purple-gray sagebrush. I began watching for a place to bed down for the night, then noticed a trail of smoke that rose from a grove, and drifted south on a gentle breeze. Maybe it meant a place for us to camp. "Hey, Patch, we may have a campfire up ahead."

He glanced around, looking in the distance, then back up at me with a look that said, *Not sure what you're talking about.*

We headed off the trail, working our way through the stand of trees. As we neared a small meadow, where the smoke came from, I heard, "Hold it, right there."

I looked off to my left, the direction of the voice, and saw a man standing behind a large boulder in among the trees. He was holding a shotgun against his hip, aimed right at me.

"Easy, friend," I said, stopping Blaze. Patch was locked in on him, voicing his low growl. "It's okay, Patch."

I glanced back at the guy with the gun, and said, "We're not looking for any kind of trouble, mister."

He lowered his shotgun, and stepped from behind the boulder. "I'm not lookin' for any either. Just making sure none was coming my way."

I swung down from Blaze, and extended my hand to him. He stepped closer to shake it, saying, "I'm Carl Grayson."

"Troy MacAlan. Call me Mack. That's Patch nosing toward you."

He reached down, scratched behind Patch's ears, and said, "Hey Patch." Patch sat in front of him, and raised his head with a look of, *You can continue with that. No need to stop right now.*

"Mind if we share your fire for the night?" I asked.

"Not at all," he replied. "Glad fer da compnee."

I unsaddled Blaze, and propped the saddle against a rock near the campfire. I led her to a nearby clearing, where she could graze and rest for the night, then took her bridle off. Untying my bedroll, I spread the ground sheet and laid the blanket over it. I plopped down on the blanket, and leaned back against the saddle to relax a bit. Patch walked over, and laid next to me.

I saw what looked like two birds strung on a long branch over the fire, and asked Carl, "What'cha got cookin'? Smells mighty good."

"Prairie chickens. Came on a bunch of 'em back a ways, and picked-off two. You're sure welcome t' join me. Dey're almost done, and don't think I can eat more 'n one of 'em mysef."

"Thanks, I'll take you up on that. I can save what I got in my kit for tomorrow's trip into Carson City."

The birds were tasty and juicy. I shared a few bites with Patch, who looked up at me brightly, as if to say, *Why can't we eat this good all the time?*

Relaxed with full stomachs, darkness began to settle over us. Soon, we drifted off for the night.

At daybreak, I was awakened by a sound I recognized, even in my sleepy haze. It was the metallic click of the hammer of a revolver being cocked.

Startled, I raised my head, and saw Carl standing in front of me, his Smith and Wesson aimed at my chest.

"What are you doing?" I croaked, my voice still thick from sleep.

"Got no choice," was his answer.

"No choice? You got lots of choices. This ain't one of the good ones."

"Move on over t' dat tree," he said, waving his gun. "Sit wit' yer back agin' it."

"What's this about, Carl?"

"Jus' git on over," he snarled, and waved the gun with more agitation.

I slowly walked over to the tree, and turned to sit. When he came toward me, his gun in one hand and rope in the other, I saw a blur from the corner of my eye. Patch was airborne, and hit Carl in the shoulder, knocking him to his knee, then over on his side. I dove on him, trying to land with my full weight to pin him down, then grabbed for his gun hand.

He tried to struggle, so I released my right hand, and hit him hard in the face with my elbow. I heard a painful moan, and he briefly stopped his struggle. I quickly grabbed the gun, wrenching it from his grip. He struggled to get up, so I elbowed him hard in the stomach, trying to keep him focused on pain.

I stood up and backed away, as he shook his head, trying to clear his thoughts. Then he raised himself to look up at me. "Now it's your turn," I told him. "You move over and sit against that tree."

He lifted up on an elbow, and Patch, who'd been locked in on him since knocking him to the ground, started his low growl.

"It's okay, Patch. Come on over here," I said, slapping the side of my thigh. He moved, and sat near me, but was still locked on Carl.

I tied Carl's wrists together behind the tree. Then, emptying his Smith & Wesson, I laid it, and the bullets, on his blanket. I sat back down on my blanket and glared at him a few moments. "I can't figure it. You some kind of road agent... set people up, then rob 'em?"

He hung his head, remaining silent. I prodded more, asking, "What's your story, Carl?"

After more silence, he looked up, asking, "Ya really want muh story, or jis gonna haul me in?"

It was my turn for silence. I studied him a while, then asked, "So, there's a story behind this?"

"You may not t'ink so. But, yeah, der is."

I continued to stare at him, and he hung his head again. This time with a greater sense of shame, and reddened eyes. I wondered what this could be about, and eventually said, "Okay, let's hear it... all of it. "

Chapter Eighteen

"I'm an eastern Kentuckian, 'n got a hunnert 'n sixty acre hardscrabble place back der. My wife 'n two boys are runnin' it. Boys are fourteen and fifteen... good sized, and able to help muh Amy run da place. I came out heah late las' fall, hopin' like mose t' hit me a gold strike. I reckoned to be back by August, else send money to bring 'em all out dis-a-way if'n ah got lucky.

"Ah tol' Amy t' write me in Carson City. Den, a few months back, ah moved ova t' Nevada City, 'n was prospectin' a small area dat weren't already overrun wit' other miners. Meantime, ah jis plum fergot t' be checkin' back at the Carson City Post Office, case Amy wrote. 'Bout a week and a half back, it come to me to check on the mail. Got that thar letter in muh saddlebag." He nodded in the direction of his saddle.

"The oldest boy, Seth, was patchin' the roof on our barn, when he fell trew a couple rotten boards. Landed on his back 'cross the side of a stall 'n busted hisse'f up bad. Amy had to spend most all o' what we had on surgeries 'n treatments. He's a good boy, 'n we'd spend our last nickel tryin' to patch him up. Dat put her gettin' way behind at da bank. When she wrote, we only had t'ree months left t' catch up wit' da bank, else lose our place. Da letter had been sittin' at da post office fer a month 'n a half, so I'm gonna be right down t' da nub tryin' t' save it. It's wirt' nearly ten times what we owe t' catch up, so...."

I got up, and stepped over to his saddle. "This bag?" I asked, pointing.

"No, t'other. You'll find da letter from her, and a nice pitchur of muh family."

I found the small portrait, wrapped in the letter, and sat back down. I read what she wrote, then looked at the picture. As I re-read the letter again, I absently stroked Patch's shoulder. When I glanced down at him, he raised his head from his outstretched paws with a cautious look that said, *I'm not sure either.*

"So, why didn't you just ask for help?"

"I have, jis 'bout everywhere ah could. Mah friends, acquaintances, banks... 'n ah cain't blame da folks. Dey hardly know this fool Kentuckian, and uh'm askin' for a good bit o' hep."

"How much?"

"Payments t' catch us up, den 'nough money fer one more surgery Seth needs... be mighty near two hunnert 'n ninety bucks. Best part of a year's wages fer most hard workin' folk."

I looked at the picture again, then got up. I untied the rope from his wrists, and threw it toward his saddle. Then I handed him his picture, saying, "Don't try anything like that again. You may end up dead."

He nodded, walked over to sit on his blanket, then told me, "Finally figgered t' do whatever it took t' git da money... cheat, steal, rob, anathin' uh had t' do. Den uh'd worry 'bout repayin' and makin' t'ings right, later. But uh would make t'ings right"

He dug in his bag, then reached to show me the envelope that his wife had mailed the letter in. On the back he'd scribbled, *Troy MacAlan, Eagle Bluff.*

"What's that?" I asked.

"I writ dat dis mornin'. Figgered t' give back what uh took... somehow, some way. Uh know it don't make it right, but what would you do?"

Just what would I do? I wondered. I stared over at Blaze, who had remained calm through all of this. I know I'd do an awful lot just to protect Blaze and Patch. What about family? Family... that vague memory for me.

I fished in my saddlebag for the small sack of oats and walked over to Blaze. I stood feeding her a few big handfuls, and wondered what to do about Carl and his problems. Soon, I found myself sitting and staring at Carl. He had an uneasy look of concern, probably wondering what was gonna happen.

I said, "Instead of turning you over to the Sheriff — that's what I *should* do — I'm gonna do what feels right. I want you to meet me in Eagle Bluff. Be there Tuesday afternoon... about three o'clock.

"I'm riding over to Carson City on business for a couple of days, but will be back to Eagle Bluff by mid-afternoon Tuesday. Meet me at the Territorial Bank. You'll have to wait if I'm running behind.

"We're going to meet with Mr. Bray. We'll see if they can telegraph two hundred and ninety dollars from my account to your wife in Kentucky.

"If not, I'll get cash, and you'll have to high-tail it back home. I'm giving you an extra twenty dollars, either way, to get you home."

Understandably, he didn't know what to say. Then he offered, "One day, Ah'll pay it back. Don't know how else t' thank yuh."

"It's not a loan. You don't have to repay it. The only way for you to say thanks, is some day, when you're able, you give a helping hand to someone who needs it. Then you'll have satisfied your obligation."

He smiled, red eyed, then whispered, "Thanks."

"See you on Tuesday," I said.

Chapter Nineteen

I left Carl at his campfire. He was planning to stay one more night, then work his way toward Eagle Bluff to meet me Tuesday afternoon.

Patch, Blaze and I were headed west, and soon would be passing the Nevada State Prison. I was hoping Warden Fitzig was in his office, and that he'd be willing to see me for a short visit.

At the prison, I found the main offices, and told the receptionist I was there to see Warden Fitzig. "I don't have an appointment, but hoped the Warden could see me for just a few minutes."

"You are...?"

Instantly, I realized my name, to them, would be meaningless. "Deputy Sheriff Troy MacAlan from Eagle Bluff," I said. *Well almost anyway*, I thought.

She came back from the Warden's office, saying, "He'll see you in just a short while." Then she returned to her desk.

I thanked her, and took a seat in one of the chairs along the wall. Noticing the plaque on her desk, I asked, "Are you Carmen?"

"Yes I am, Mr. MacAlan."

"Nice meeting you, Carmen. Please call me Mack."

"Thank you, Mack."

I let her get back to her paperwork, and waited for her to look up again. When she did, I asked, "Did you know the prisoner Conner Kennedy? He was an inmate here last year."

"No, not really. Other than seeing him at those times he met with Warden Fitzig, I didn't know him."

"I wondered if he was as nasty as I've heard. Sounded like he caused more than his share of trouble." I was probing to see what she might know.

"I really couldn't say," she answered. "As many times as he was in here, I never really spoke with him."

In a short while, as promised, a gentleman in a gray,double-breasted suit walked toward me, saying, "Deputy MacAlan?"

"Yes," I said, standing to shake his hand. He was a man in his fifties, I guessed, with a stocky build, and a firm handshake. "Call me Mack."

"Call me Fitz. How can I help you?"

"I was hoping you could answer a few questions about a former inmate, Conner Kennedy."

"Oh?" he said, questioningly. I noticed a slight flush in his cheeks. "Come back to my office. I'll see if I can help."

As we walked down the hall, he asked, "So, when did Stoney get a new deputy?"

"He just offered the job to me in the last couple of days." I felt a pang of guilt for my answer, or rather my incomplete answer. *Sins of omission*, I thought.

"That's good. I knew he needed to start grooming someone to fill his shoes."

He offered a chair, and I sat, asking, "How long did you have Conner Kennedy in your facility?"

He paused, rubbed his chin in thought, then said, "I should check his file to be sure, but I think it was a little less than a year before he died."

"How did he die?"

"Well, he managed to have a couple of run-ins with Ed LaRock, one of our worst inmates. Ed cornered him in the kitchen, and carved him up real bad. It was a gruesome thing."

"Sounds like it."

"It gave LaRock his third extended stay in isolation. But, for the hard-cores, even that doesn't do much."

"So, you didn't know Conner, or the Kennedy family, all that well?" I asked.

"No, not really. I had the usual orientation meeting with him when he came in, but that's about it. What are you hoping to find out?"

"Well..." I hesitated, trying to cover my concern over what he'd said about not knowing Conner, in contrast with things Carmen had said. "We're investigating the troubles that continue to happen while the Kennedys are buying ranches along Rush Creek. I was headed to Carson City on other business, so I thought I'd stop to see what light you could shed."

"Sorry, Mack, but I'm afraid I'm not much help."

"Understandable," I said, nodding. "But it was worth a try." *And, Mister Warden, you've been more help than you know*, I thought.

I stood from my chair. He came around the desk to shake my hand, then showed me to the door. "Good luck with your investigation," he said.

Outside, Patch saw me and sat up, his tail brushing the ground excitedly. *It's nice being missed so much*, I thought, then bent to tussle with him, scratching his neck and shoulders. "Okay, Patch, next stop is dinner."

On the way into Carson City, I found a gentle slope leading down to the Carson River, where I could water and feed them.

After they'd quenched their thirst, I led them over to a stretch of grass, and put out some dog food for Patch. When I figured they'd eaten enough, I said, "Okay guys, time to find an eatery, so I can get some dinner."

Soon, I was sitting in Doug's Diner, where a waitress, with beautiful red hair, introduced herself as Liz. When she smiled her bright smile, it narrowed her eyes to mere slits, and gave her a very sweet look. I asked her if she knew where I could find Bill Nelson, the Assay Agent.

She explained where his office was, then added, "He's usually back from dinner by one-thirty."

She was right. I sat on the edge of the boardwalk in front of his office, and, at one-twenty-five, a man stopped to unlock the door.

"Bill Nelson?" I asked.

"Yup." Then, pausing before he stepped in the door, he said, "Come on in, Mr...?"

"Troy MacAlan. Deputy from Eagle Bluff."

"Come on in, Deputy MacAlan."

Following him, I said, "Please, call me Mack."

"I didn't know they had hired a new Deputy in Eagle Bluff yet, Mack," he said, as he closed the door behind us. "'Course I haven't seen Stoney in weeks."

"Actually, Stoney just asked me if I wanted the job a couple of days ago." *Guilt again.* "We're investigating the troubles surrounding the Kennedys, as they've been buying up ranches along Rush Creek. I wondered if you had any gold dealings with them, or anyone else, that might be from Rush Creek."

He sat down at his desk. "Well, I remember a time Brendan came in to have some ore assayed, probably a year and a half ago. At the time, I think he told me it was from somewhere along the Carson River, but he's not been back since."

He stared blankly for a while, slowly scratching his temple, then said, "Next thing I remember is Conner coming in with some. He also said it was from near the Carson River. It assayed out about the same as what Brendan had brought in."

"You think their stories were true?"

"Well, I've sometimes wondered if they'd found a placer. That's how Brendan first made his gold strike a few years back."

"Okay... " I said, pausing in thought. "So, there is the possibility that he's found something, and just hasn't told anyone about it."

"Don't hold me to it, but I'd say there's a pretty fair possibility."

"Well, Bill, I thank you for your time. You've been very helpful. Eventually, all of these bits of information will begin to tie together."

"I sure hope so," he said. "For everyone's sake."

"I do, too," I said, reaching for the door.

Back outside, I sat on the edge of the boardwalk, my loyal sidekick at my side. I sorted through the questions about Warden Fitzig. Might he be connected with Conner's death? Is he connected with the Kennedys? He had lots of sessions with Conner, then claimed he didn't really know him, or see him more than a time or two... he's got to be involved somehow. Did he arrange for LaRock to do him in? What's he trying to cover up?

Then there's all the open questions about Brendan Kennedy. Could he have been involved in Conner's death? Did he find gold? Maybe discovered a placer? Were he and his boys behind all the trouble?

"Interesting," I said, looking at Patch. He rested his head on his outstretched paws, not seeming to be all that interested.

Chapter Twenty

There were a few more stops I had to make, then we'd have an early supper, and head back east. We could put a few hours behind us, find the Kentuckian's campsite, spend the night there, then ride the rest of the way back to Eagle Bluff tomorrow.

A couple hours later, with everyone fed and watered, we headed east. The late afternoon sun warmed my back. Following the Carson River for a while, we picked up the wagon trail we'd come in on.

Soon, I began noticing heavy storm clouds gathering in the northwest sky, far behind us. It didn't look any too promising. "It's bad news, Blaze," I said. "Storm's movin' faster'n we are. We're likely to get real wet tonight."

We left the river terrain, and worked our way into the rugged, rocky, sagebrush range. There wasn't much point to pick up the pace, since we couldn't outrun the storm. The wind blew stronger against my back, and the heavy dark clouds were moving in. It was lookin' more 'n more like it was gonna be a gully washer, and I wondered when it might open up on us.

I felt a sudden stir of strong wind, and tugged my hat down tighter on my head. When I felt rain slap against my cheek, I reached back for my slicker. Struggling to get it on, fighting the strong winds, I stood in the stirrups and pulled the slicker under me. I sat back down, and tucked it around my legs, foolishly hoping that it would keep the seat of my pants dry.

I decided to keep to the low ground, trying to avoid lightning strikes that usually hit trees on higher ground. The last of the evening light had been snuffed out by the storm clouds and, suddenly, much stronger winds and a heavy downpour opened up on us. Lightning snapped and flashed, and loud thunder rolled all around us. We continued on into the teeth of it, struggling to see our way in the brief flashes of lightning. With no place to hole up, we had to fight on through the storm.

A while later, I could see we were passing the wide mouth of a ravine that ran far back up the slope to the high rocky buttes. The ground at the mouth was already soaked and soft from a stream of water weaving its way down the ravine.

I noticed Patch and Blaze perk up, and I glanced around, wondering... then I heard it. The loud roar told me there was a wall of water crashing down the ravine toward us. I knew we had to get to higher ground, and get there in a big hurry.

I strained to see through the darkness and heavy rain, hoping for more lightning. Then, in a series of flashes, I saw a gradual slope on the far side of the ravine. It led up to a plateau. "C'mon Patch," I shouted, as I leaned forward and spurred Blaze in the flanks. In an instant, she was galloping up the slope, dancing through rocks and small trees. As we reach the plateau, I eased her to a stop, then turned her toward the ravine to watch.

Not twenty seconds later, a wall of water thundered down the ravine. In the flashes of lightning I could see dead logs and uprooted trees being carried in the fierce, churning wall of water. Dumping out into the open low land, the fury of the flash flood was ferocious and frightening. Then it quickly defused.

Patch, standing near and watching it all, looked up at me. "Thanks for the warning," I said to him. His head tilted, and his ears perked up.

"You too, girl," I said to Blaze, leaning forward to pat her on the neck. "We've gotta find shelter. This could be an all-nighter." We backtracked down the slope, and picked up the trail we'd been on, which was a little more soggy and sloppy now. I studied the terrain and the slopes ahead, as lightning gave opportunity. *Something... an overhanging rock ledge, a cave, a grove of trees... anything to get relief from the downpour*, I thought, straining to see through the pounding rain.

Then, just as a lightning flash was fading, something caught my eye. "C'mon," I whispered, wanting another flash that would light up the slope far off to our left.

Then, in the brightness of another lightning bolt, I saw it again. It looked like an abandoned wood shack, sitting up on a large plateau.

"We may be in luck, Patch," I said, as I nudged Blaze into a trot. I spotted a trail heading up to the plateau, and it brought us right to the shack. As we neared, I could see that the walls were missing a few boards. It was a dirt floor shack, maybe twelve feet wide by sixteen feet long. I felt some relief when I could see the roof intact, and the floor dry... mostly. It had an overhang that likely covered a nice porch at one time. I dismounted, and tied Blaze under it.

"Good girl," I said, scratching her cheeks. Then I knelt and stroked Patch. "And you, too," I said, smiling at him. "You guys saved our hides." He looked up at me, glad that I understood.

99

I peeked inside the shack, glad to see the roof was still solid. A little rain blew through gaps in the walls, but it was a welcome shelter. I grabbed my bedroll, and stepped inside. Against a wall, I saw a wooden bench, and the remains of a wood table. *Dry wood*, I thought.

Splintering a few pieces of the broken table, we soon had the makin's of a small fire. Sheltered from the heavy rain, and feeling the warmth of the fire, comfort soon began to displace the cold, wet, tension of the evening's turmoil.

I spread my ground sheet and blanket near the fire. Then I sat on the bench, and struggled to pull off my wet boots. I set them above the fire on a cross-brace for the roof rafters. Hopefully, they'd be nearly dry by morning. I did the same with my hat, vest, shirt, Levi's, and socks. It wasn't a real cold night, so layin' undressed in my wool blanket near the fire, I'd be comfortable. I decided to leave the saddle on Blaze. It was more likely to dry some up there on her back, then it would lying on the ground.

As I lay wrapped in the blanket, feeling warm and comfortable, I thought about Carl. *How was he weathering this night.* The next thing I was conscious of, was feeling a chill, and opening my eyes to see only the glowing embers of the fire. I stoked it to a strong flame, adding enough wood to carry us until morning... I hoped.

Chapter Twenty-One

The next time I opened my eyes, I saw the faint, early glow of dawn. "Hey, the storm has passed," I said to Blaze and Patch, who were already alert. I stoked the fire once again, saying, "Might as well take the edge off the cool morning air." I wondered if they tire of me talking to them. "No, I don't think you tire of it at all," I said, as they looked at me curiously.

I grabbed the bag of dog food, and put a couple handfuls on the ground for Patch. Then I took the small sack of sweet oats from the feed mill in Carson City, and fed Blaze several handfuls. Finally, I opened my pouch of jerked beef, and took out a few pieces for my breakfast. Washing it down with water from my canteen, I said, "After that storm, we'll find plenty of water for you guys to drink when we hit the trail."

My clothes were dry, and I didn't mind that my boots were still damp. Having boots dry as you wear 'em always gives a good "form fit." The saddle was still a little damp, too, so to avoid a wet seat all day, I folded my blanket to use as a dry cushion. I led Blaze from under the roof, and swung into the saddle. Giving a last glance toward the fire I'd doused, we headed down the slope, then caught the trail east to Eagle Bluff.

It was nearing four o'clock when we rode into town, and I saw Carl patiently waiting on the bench in front of the bank. When he saw us round the corner at the hotel, he stood and waved. I walked Blaze up to the hitching rail and, as I wrapped the reins, asked Carl, "So, how did you whether that storm last night?"

"None too good," he answered, slowly shaking his head. "Ah was wet da whole night."

"Don't look wet now," I said, giving him a once-over.

"Not so bad. Da ride back t' town, 'den sittin' here, perched in da sun and warm breeze, hepped dry me off a good bit. How 'bout yerse'f... don't look none da worse fer it all."

I explained about getting caught out in the open, and how we eventually found the shack. "And the ride today has dried us, too, for the most part." We visited more about the fierce battle with the storm, then I said, "Let's go inside, and see if they can help us."

We walked in the bank, and the teller asked us to have a seat until Mr. Bray finished with his current customer. Before long, Bray walked his customer to the door, then turned to us. "Hello, Mr. MacAlan," he said, stepping over to shake our hands.

"Call me Mack," I told him, as I shook his hand.

"Mack it is," he agreed, then turned to shake Carl's as I introduced them.

"Please, come on over to my desk," he said, waving for us to follow. We sat, and I explained what we wanted to have him do. He told us he could help.

"Even way out here in Nevada, we're able to do business all over the country in only a few days. We can telegraph to the bank in Kentucky, and it should be available to your wife within three days."

We finished our business with Tom, and went back out on the boardwalk. I fished in my vest pocket, and brought out one of the three gold pieces I still had in there. Reaching toward him, I said, "Here's the twenty dollars I told you I'd give you. That should get you back home."

He took the coin, stared at it for a long moment, then clutched it tightly and looked up. "Uh know we talked 'bout dis, but uh jus' can't begin t' tell ya how much dis means t' muh family."

I felt a soft smile forming. "I do know that you're grateful. And, like I mentioned, you can show it when you're able to help someone who desperately needs it." He looked me in the eye a long while, then nodded.

To lighten things, I asked, "Are you going to send your wife a telegram? Tell her she can pay the bank, and the doctor?"

"Uh surely am, Mack... soon's we're done here. An' uh been a-thinkin' some 'bout da trip home, too. Uh'm fixin' t' sell muh horse 'n saddle, den catch da stagecoach back t' Carson City. From thar, Uh'll take the next railroad back t' Louisville, where kinfolk'll pick me up. Be back home in a week, 'stead of a month on horseback."

"Sounds like you've got the right idea. Be sure to tell your family hello for me, and wish them all the best."

"You kin count on it, Mack."

Chapter Twenty-Two

I left Carl, and headed for the Sheriff's office. As he heard the door open, Stoney dropped his feet from his desktop, and sat up quickly. "Oh... howdy, Mack. Caught me in my late afternoon catnap," he said, showing a little flush in his cheeks.

"Sorry for my bad timing," I told him, grinning.

"Not a problem at all. A fella's got a right to a nap now and again."

"No argument from me."

"C'mon in. Have a seat." He pointed for me to pull up a chair, as he began to straighten his desk. "What'cha doin' in town this afternoon?"

"Just back from a trip I made over to Carson City. I had an interesting visit with Warden Fitzig at the prison. Then I stopped to see Bill Nelson, the Assay Agent for their area."

"Did you learn anything from them?"

"Yes, I did. Well... sort of anyway," I said, with a shrug.

"And?" he said slowly, as he brought out his fixin's, and rolled a cigarette. He struck a match, and took a deep drag to light the tobacco. Motioning with his tobacco pouch, he asked, "Don't use, do ya?"

I held up a hand, saying, "Nope, I don't."

"Anyway..." he drawled, opening the door for me to continue with what I was saying.

"Anyway, there were some interesting contradictions from Fitzig. I visited with his secretary as I waited for the Warden. She said Conner Kennedy had met with him on quite a number of occasions. Then Fitzig tried to make it sound like there'd been nothing more than his usual orientation meeting with Conner.

"So..." I continued. "What's he hiding? Did he have something to do with Conner's death? Was he involved with Brendan Kennedy? Is there gold he's interested in? Just a passel of new questions."

"And, so far, no good answers I suppose," he said, while watching the smoke roll up from his cigarette.

"No, not yet. Then I met with Bill Nelson, who added more to the list of unanswered questions."

He shifted, getting himself more comfortable, while I continued. "First he had a visit from Brendan about a year and a half ago. Brought in some ore he said was from somewhere along the Carson River. Then, just a short while later, Conner came in with a small amount of similar grade ore. He also claimed it was from the Carson River. Finally, after Conner was in prison, Fitzig came in with a small bit of ore. He said it was given to him by a friend. Are these all just coincidences?"

He showed a sly grin. "No, it don't strike me that way. And, I'll bet, it don't you either."

"Nope. How it fits together... now that's the puzzle."

He blew a smoke ring and watched it drift toward the window, while he considered these new questions. Soon the ring drifted apart, and a wave of smoke floated through the sunlight coming in the window. "That's gonna take some pondering," he said, looking back at me.

"Let me know if anything comes to mind." I pushed my chair back, stood, then hesitated. "Oh, by the way, if anyone asks, I did introduce myself as your new deputy. I figured it would help open the doors over there in Carson City. So...."

He smiled broadly. "No problem, Deputy MacAlan."

I waved, shut the door, and stood on the boardwalk looking at my loyal companions. "Let's head for the Witten ranch," I said, then added, "Patch, let's go find Stumpy." He looked at me, head tilted, then jumped down from the boardwalk and waited while I grabbed the reins, and swung up on Blaze.

I told the Wittens we'd be back for supper on Tuesday, and we were right on schedule. We headed west toward some good home-cooked food, and a comfortable bed. The sun was warm on my face, and there was a gentle breeze that felt cool and fresh. It felt good to be alive. It felt good to have helped Carl and his family with all their troubles. I felt so good in fact, that I let loose with a song called The Utah Trail, and was singin' so's to be heard at the top of the distant buttes. I thought I was soundin' pretty good, too, until Blaze's ears twitched. Then Patch slowed to look up at me with a curious tilt to his head. I paused, mid-chorus, and asked, "That bad, huh? Alright then. I'll just relax and soak up the sun." They both seemed relieved.

When we reached the ranch, Stumpy came over to say hello, and was petting Patch, who had run ahead to greet him. As we talked, I scooped a dish of food for Patch and grain for Blaze, then I brushed her down.

After a time, Stumpy said, "While you were gone, we had another dose of trouble come our way."

"What happened this time?"

"Well, actually, it was more of the same. This time someone tore down a long section of the north fence line. A hundred head of cattle were scattered hell-to-breakfast, and we were riding all day yesterday 'n better part of today roundin' 'em up."

"Soooo... more fence work."

"Yup," he groaned. "There'll likely be three or four days' worth this go-round."

Chapter Twenty-Three

When Stump and I walked in for supper, I got a firm handshake and "Howdy" from Will. Then I got a friendly hug and "Hello" from Julie. We sat to eat, and they wanted to hear all about my journey to Carson City, and what I'd found out.

I told them of meeting Carl, the storm, then finally helping him and his family.

"That's a good thing you did," Julie said, brightly.

Stumpy nodded. "A real stand-up thing, after the guy tried to bushwhack you."

I told them of my conversations with Warden Fitzig and Bill Nelson, and all the questions that were raised. "The only help, I reckon, is that it gives us some things we can dig a little deeper into."

That night, as I stretched out on my bunk, I said to Stumpy, "It don't take many nights livin' on the ground to make a body appreciate a comfortable bed."

He chuckled. "Dun got that right. G'night Mack." He turned down the lamp, and was purring in moments.

Next morning, we headed to the north fence line. For several hours things were going along just fine as we dug and set posts. Then, suddenly, Stumpy winced and put a hand to his back. He stayed bent over and motionless.

"What happened, Stump?"

"I-I-I did it again," he groaned. "Twanged somethin'
in my back." He put his hands on his knees, trying to take
the pressure off his back. As he tried to straighten, he
flinched, and I could see the pain in his face. He slowly rose
a bit, then grabbed hold of my shoulder.

I helped him to the wagon, and he wiggled onto the
bed. "Maybe laying flat will help," I said. When he was far
enough on, he rolled onto his back

"Could you prop your saddle bags under my legs?" he
asked. "It might give some relief."

"Has this happened before, Stump?"

"Yeah, over the past few years I've managed to tweak
it a couple of times. Soon it'll ease up, and I'll begin to feel
okay. Then it might not bother me for another year...
sometimes even longer."

"Rest here, and try to relax your back. I'm gonna get
back to diggin' and settin' posts until Will comes with our
dinner."

"Thanks, Mack," he said, trying to grin, and not show
his pain.

Patch followed me back to where I'd left the shovel,
and watched as I started digging post holes again. The tall
sagebrush nearby gave him shade, and he stretched out,
relaxing in the coolness. As I moved post to post, he moved
with me, finding more shady areas to lie in. When I noticed
him perk up, I turned and saw Will riding toward us in the
distance. I pulled the bandana from my pocket, and dried
my face and forehead. Then I wiped around the inside of my
hat.

"It's dinner time, Patch," I said. "Where's Stumpy?"

He rose to his feet in one fluid motion, then looked from me to the wagon. "That's right. Go find Stumpy."

He hesitated, glancing back and forth again. "Go on, boy... go find Stumpy," I repeated. He jogged over to the wagon, jumped up on the bed, and lay beside him.

"Good boy, Patch," I said, as I walked to the wagon. I reached to pet him and scratch behind his ears, then saw Stump's eyes open. He reached to pet Patch, too.

"You're such a good dog, Patch," he whispered. Patch stretched to lick Stump's chin, which made him laugh and wince in pain.

"C'mon Patch. Jump down here," I said, motioning toward the shade under the wagon. "Let Stumpy relax."

Will rode up, and knew right away what was wrong. "You twang your back again, Stump?"

"Yeah... somehow I managed to do it again."

He swung down from the saddle, and took sandwiches from his saddle bag. "Can you eat a sandwich while you lie there on your back?"

"Oh, I think so," he answered, the pain still showing in his voice.

As we ate, Will said, "Think I'll bring him back to the house in the wagon, and help him onto his bunk. Usually, after a day or two of rest, those muscles loosen up, and he's back in business."

That evening, as I rode up to the house, I saw Stoney on the front porch with Will and Julie. All three waved as I came around the barn.

Julie called Patch's name. "C'mere boy... c'mere... I got a treat." He loped toward her, his whole body showing how excited he was. She gave him some beef scraps from the roast she'd cooked for supper, and he cleaned the plate in about ten seconds. Then he wagged his whole body, looking up at her for more.

"That's all for now," she said, as she sat back in her chair. He moved to lay beside her, holding his head high, proud as you please.

"Maybe one day you'll have someone to pamper you that way," Stoney joked, looking my way.

"You think?" I sighed, with sarcasm. I pulled up a chair, and asked, "How's Stumpy doin'?"

"Better," Will said. "He thinks he can join us for supper. But I think he'll have to lay low tomorrow. At least for the morning."

"So what brings you out, Stoney?" I asked, shifting my attention to him.

"Come to ask a favor," he said, as he rolled the short butt of his cigarette between his thumb and forefinger, squeezing out the flame. Then he tucked the butt in the cuff of his jeans.

I glanced at Will and Julie, then back to Stoney. "What kind of favor?"

"Well, since it seems I'm now covering your rump for impersonating an officer of the law," he drawled, shooting a sly grin toward the Wittens, "I thought maybe you could return the favor by serving as the real Deputy MacAlan for the next couple days."

I leaned back in my chair, grinning myself now, and asked, "Just what is it you need help with?"

"There's a big cattle drive comin' through our area. It's happened a couple times before, and things have gotten a little out of hand. This one has about three thousand head, with probably eighteen drovers. I think they're headed for Colorado.

"North of town a few miles, there's a huge grassy area with Sand Creek winding its way through it. It's the perfect spot for them to lay-over a few days, and let the cattle graze and water... keep 'em fat and healthy while they're on the trail."

"And you need my help for...."

"Help keep things from gettin' out of control in town again... like before. They'll be laying over two, maybe three days. At night they'll leave four or five behind to ride herd, while the others come to town and let loose. After a couple weeks of sittin' a horse, herdin' cattle and eatin' dust, you can't blame 'em for wantin' to kick it up some. But, sometimes things get a little crazy. You've got the kind of temperament to douse the fires, keep them calmed down and under control."

I hesitated, looking down at Patch. Finally, I said, "Okay, I'll help. When do you want me?"

"I thought you could come over to my office on Wednesday, before supper, and I can swear you in and give you a badge. The wages are a dollar 'n a half per day, and we'll pay your room and meals at the hotel. Monday morning you can head back to your job here."

I glanced at Will and Julie, and assumed Stoney had explained this already, as I saw no objection showing on their faces.

Will spoke up. "I think Stoney's right. You're the man he needs."

"I'll be there at five o'clock on Wednesday," I said, with a nod at Stoney.

"Glad to hear it, Mack. Maybe we can give Doc Undahl a little rest this year. Last fall she had to treat a passel of busted hands, and some busted heads from all the brawling. She even treated two or three bullet wounds. Hopefully, we can keep the roosters from so much hookin' and clawin' this time around."

Chapter Twenty-Four

Wednesday I walked into Stoney's office to be sworn in as deputy, and get a badge pinned to my vest. After making it official, he sat behind his desk, saying, "Pull up a chair. Let's talk about how we're going to handle things."

As I sat, I took a folded paper from my shirt pocket. "I've got an idea I picked up in Carson City. I think it could make it a whole lot easier to keep things under rein. But we need Town Council approval behind it to make it work."

"What'cha got in mind?"

"Well, I wrote this up from memory, so we may need to refine it some." I handed him the paper. It read:

By Order of Eagle Bluff Town Council and Sheriff Stoney Dawson

No guns shall be drawn or discharged within town limits.

No fighting or abusive conduct will be tolerated.

Disorderly drunks will be arrested and put in jail.

Repeat offenders will be escorted out of town, or jailed.

He read it, then read it a second time. He raised his eyes, and looked at me thoughtfully. "I like it. It's time we get a little more organized in our town." Laying it on his desk, he rolled and lit a cigarette. Watching the smoke rise, he mulled it over in his mind. I waited, letting him think it through.

"You're right about getting the Town Council behind it. I can get word to all but one of 'em. He's over in Virginia City for a few days. The rest could gather after supper, and take action on this."

"Think any would object?"

"No. And if one did, I'd offer him the job of ridin' herd on this town for the next four days."

"I'm gonna walk down to ask Dave at the Gazette if he'll print up a couple dozen of these before he closes up his shop for the night," I said. "We can run some more if there's any changes."

"Good idea. I'll get them gathered for an emergency meeting after supper."

At seven o'clock, the four councilmen were in Stoney's office. Dave Long had been more than happy to print the flyers up for us. I gave each councilman a copy as they arrived. When they were all present, Stoney began the meeting.

"You're lookin' at the purpose of this special meeting this evening," he said, waving a copy of the flyer. "I'd like you to consider passing this into town ordinance, so we can enforce it with legal authority." He paused, looking toward each of them.

One of the councilman, who Stoney later told me is always contrary, asked him, "Why do you think we need more ordinances like these? We already have plenty of good laws to be enforced."

Stoney paused, looking at the flyer he held, then looked at the councilman. "Well, Abraham, if a man shoots you, assaults you, robs you, or steals your horse... I have a law to stop him, and can arrest him. I don't have a law to stop other kinds of bad behavior.

"And, if you think back, you've been right in there with those who are fed up with the bullying ways of some men, the mean drunk ways of others, and even those who like to pull their gun whenever they please. Ordinances like these being proposed would give us the authority to stop all that crazy stuff."

"He's right, Abe," another councilman said. "You know how much we've complained about being more and more afraid to go to the saloon on any evening. If Stoney thinks this will help him clean things up, I'm all for it. It'd be nice to feel at ease in a saloon again."

Stoney glanced at the others, then asked, "Any more questions or objections?" He gave them time to consider it, then said, "Since there's none, I'd like to see a formal motion passing these into law."

Tom Bray, the bank vice president, spoke up, saying, "I move we adopt these into town ordinance. And, if no one objects, I'll act as recording secretary for the council in John's absence. That's part of the motion, too, and I'll write it all down."

Abraham, with a change of heart, said, "I second it."

All voted in favor of the motion, then Stoney thanked them for their help. "Now, you can go back home to your families, comfortable that things are going to get a mite bit better."

When they had left, he looked at me, saying, "Now, that was a right good idea. I think it'll help change things in a big hurry."

"I thought the same," I said. "Seeing these posted when I was in Carson City, I asked their Sheriff about them. He said the idea was borrowed from a Kansas town that had become an out-and-out rustlers' roost, full of thugs and outlaws doing whatever they wanted. This helped take back their town. Need the men to enforce it, but it cleaned up their town right well."

"I think we've got the men to back it up," he said, tapping the flyer on his desk. "Along with you and me, we got Big Jake. He sometimes serves as a Deputy, and will be helping us for the next few days." Glancing at his watch, he added, "He should be here any time now... with his sawed-off double barrel."

My eyes popped open, and I stuttered. "Th... that mountain of a man, holding a cut-off shotgun? Now, that would get your attention."

"You can bet it does. And it's a ten gauge Parker. There's a mite few men that can cipher past two times ten, when lookin' up those quarter-size ten gauge barrels. And with Jake carrying it, any man set on makin' trouble tends to quiet right down."

Laughing, I turned to see Big Jake walk in.

118

"What's so funny?" his booming voice snarled, then he gave us a big grin.

"C'mon in Jake," Stoney said. "Grab a chair. I've got something to show you."

As Jake spun a chair around to sit, he asked, "How're you doin', Mack?"

"Just fine, Jake. And you?"

"Well, my toe's been giving me grief these past few days. And my pinky finger here, it's been a pain since I brushed it across a hot shoe. And..."

He paused, and looked up from his finger. "Oh... maybe you didn't really want all the details." He shrugged, let loose with his hardy laugh, then asked, "How 'bout you, Sheriff?"

"Well, you know, this knee of mine..." Stoney began, then glanced up at Jake.

"Okay now..." Jake said, chuckling.

"We've just finished with a quick meeting of the Town Council," Stoney told him. "Got some new stuff that's gonna help considerable." He leaned to hand Jake a copy of the flyer, then sat back while he read it.

"You're right," Jake says, looking up from the flyer. "This is gonna help us out a whole lot."

"Mack's idea," Stoney said. "It'll give the trouble makers a whole new chunk of meat to chew on. For the first time we'll have a law behind us if they're raisin' hell."

Jake leaned back in his chair, and crossed a leg over. "Quite an idea there, Mack."

"Thanks," I said, then looked at Stoney. "Don't want to rattle things too much, but I've got another suggestion for you to consider."

He stared at me for a moment, then said, "So... let's hear it."

I hesitated, looked at each of them again, then asked, "What would you think about deputizing Rita to help us?"

Chapter Twenty-Five

"Ruthless Rita?" Jake asked, sounding shocked.

"I thought it was Ragin' Rita," I said.

Stoney laughed. "Well, sometimes it's both."

"I'm not so sure about that one," Jake said.

Stoney was staring thoughtfully at his hands, then finally looked up, and said, "Maybe it's not such a bad idea. She can handle herself better than half the men in this town. And it might surprise people enough to get their attention. That wouldn't be such a bad thing."

"That's what I thought when I saw her manhandle Carson in the street. Put a badge on her and rein her in a bit, she might be a big help." I sat back, waiting for more from them.

After a time, Stoney said, "I like the idea. It's too late for tonight, but I'll talk to her in the mornin'." He began to stand, saying, "I expect we'll see that pack of cow punchers in a short while. And, like always, the locals will be here marking their territory, and struttin' their stuff. Let's start posting flyers, and get ready for the dance."

As we hung the flyers up and down the boardwalks, we saw that a couple of the local ranch crews were in the saloons. Stoney figured the cow punchers would ride in from the east, past Jake's livery. "I'm sure they'll come a-hightailin'... whoopin' it up, and shootin' at the moon. Let's meet 'em at the edge of town."

We strolled down to the livery, and relaxed on chairs outside Jake's double-doors. As we sat, I noticed there was a girl, a young teenager, working an Appaloosa on a long lead rope. "Who's that?" I asked.

"My oldest daughter, Cambria," Jake said.

"She's a cute girl. Must take after her mother," I said, grinning at Jake. "And, it looks like she knows horses."

"Yes... to both. She's loved horses since she was a little tyke, and knows how to handle 'em."

I sat there watching her work. She unclipped the rope, coiled it in her hand, then moved to the center of the corral. Facing the horse, and pointing left, she said, "Walk." He turned, and began circling her at a walking pace. Soon she said, "Trot," and he picked up the pace to a nice trot. Next she said, "Lope," and he shifted gears again. Finally she said, "Whoa." He quickly stopped, then turned to face her.

She knew what she was doing all right. As she walked to him, the horse stood tall and proud. She leaned her forehead against his nose, and spoke softly to him. When she raised her head, he began nosing around her jacket pocket. She reached in the pocket, and gave him a handful of oats. I've always felt you could know a lot about a person by the way they treat animals.

Before long, we saw a rolling dust cloud, glowing red from the light of the setting sun. Watching it come closer, Stoney said, "Well boys, time we do our duty as the town's welcoming committee." He grinned, and pushed himself out of his chair. We followed his lead, taking up positions on each side of him. We were spread far enough apart to take away any thought of riding around us.

As they neared, not more than fifty yards from us, Stoney said, "Okay Jake, get their attention." That ten gauge exploded with a double blast that rattled my jawbone. Horses were rearing and bumping into one another, as riders tried to bring 'em under control. They slowed, then slid to a stop not more than twenty feet from us.

"Howdy, boys," Stoney said, as they settled. "Some of you might remember me from past visits. I'm Stoney Dawson, Sheriff of Eagle Bluff. These gentlemen here," he waved a hand, "are Deputies Jake Irving and Troy MacAlan."

"What's up with this, Sheriff?" growled a big man, who I guessed was the top hand of the bunch.

"Well, we've got some new ordinances since your last visit, so I wanted to read them to you. Get us started on the right foot. Avoid any senseless problems."

That brought a few laughs from the drovers, then one barked, "Hank, we gonna let these yocals ride roughshod over us?" He reached for the gun on his hip. Before he touched the ivory handle of his six gun, I'd cleared leather, and had my cocked revolver pointed at him, saying, "Don't touch that. Not if you would like to see the sun come up tomorrow."

At the same time, I heard Stoney lever his rifle, and Jake cock the hammers of his reloaded double barrel. The top man, who must be Hank, shouted, "Knock it off, Brock."

"That'd be a right good idea," Stoney said. "Now, if you'll listen up, I'll read the new ordinances so you all know where you stand." He read the flyer, then told 'em, "We'll be posting these around town, and in the saloons, in case you need a reminder. Now, go on ahead, and enjoy yourselves."

We stepped aside, and fourteen riders rode in a little more calmly than they otherwise would have. But they still rode up to the hitching rails fourteen strong, and walked into the saloon... fourteen strong. Ordering drinks, many were still of a mind to raise some hell. After all, that's what a break from the trail drive was all about.

The dust of riding herd lay thick on their clothes, on the back of their necks, and in their throats. Whiskey was the best way to start the cleansing process — wash the dust from your throat first, worry about the rest later.

As we watched them hitch their horses, and walk toward the saloon, Stoney blew out a big breath of air, then said, "Let's finish tacking these up along the boardwalks. After that we'll visit the saloons."

At Dusty's Saloon, we tacked a flyer on each side of the door, then another on the wall at the far end of the bar. A few of the locals stepped up to read them. Charlie spoke up, asking, "What's this? New bad boy rules?"

"You got it," Stoney snarled, when the room quieted. "So, Charlie, if you get an urge to fight, or pull that gun, it'll get you thrown in jail."

For a moment he didn't know what to say. Finally, he shook his head, saying, "Don't that beat all."

At the Eagle Bluff Saloon it didn't go quite so easy. As I stepped in and tacked flyers on each side of the door, Jake walked over to the side wall across from the bar, his sawed-off resting on his shoulder. Stoney stood next to the door with his rifle across his chest, cradled in his left elbow. A silence spread through the room, as men noticed the three of us enter the bar.

124

I walked to the far end of the bar, and tacked up a flyer. When I moved away, Hank, the top hand, stepped up and tore it from the wall. He rolled it, and held it over the chimney of a lamp. When it caught fire, he used it to light his cigarette. He stuffed the burning flyer in his nearly empty beer glass to snuff it out. Smiling at the chatter from his boys, he reached for his whiskey and downed it.

As I moved to tack up another flyer, Hank snarled, "Don't bother."

Like before in the street, Jake cocked the hammers of his shotgun, and Stoney levered his rifle. Stoney told him, "Oh, we'll bother all right. And you'll not do that again. It falls under the abusive behavior ordinance, and you'll spend a day or two resting on a jail bunk."

To Stoney's left, a chair squeaked on the floor, and the man sitting in it rose quickly to his feet. Not knowing, nor caring, what his intent was, Stoney swung the stock of his rifle. He caught the cowboy on the side of his head, stunning him, and toppling him over his chair. Watching to be sure the guy wasn't going to try anything more, he said, "Anyone else care to dance?

"So..." he continued, "Now that we all understand the new rules, you boys enjoy your drinks. Hopefully, we won't have to worry about locking anyone up for a day or two. Or worse, lock you up until our Circuit Judge comes around. Your drive may be far down the trail by then."

A heavy silence covered the saloon, like a bedroll blanket covers a cowboy for the night.

Chapter Twenty-Six

We made it through the first night with only a few skirmishes, and one injury. Oh... and one cowpuncher's severely bruised pride. That happened when he messed with Karen Zenith, once too often.

Karen provided music and entertainment at the Eagle Bluff Saloon most evenings — except Sundays, when she sang at the church morning and evening. She's a curvy woman, and a terrific piano player and singer. Her specialty is picking on cowboys, providing lots of laughs at their expense.

Tonight's victim was one of the cowpunchers who, like a young boy trying to get a girl's attention by repeatedly pulling her pigtails, kept reaching in to strike a piano key as she was playing her music. First she politely asked him to stop, then resorted to heckling him, but he still wouldn't quit. Finally, fed up with his antics, she waited and timed her revenge. Just as he reached in again, ready to strike a key, she slammed the hinged keyboard cover down hard on his finger.

The cowboy yelped, and jerked his finger back. Then he lifted his arm as though he were going to backhand her. But, when she didn't flinch, he glanced around the room and thought better of it. He stomped back to the bar, holding his finger, and his ranting ended quickly, as the other cowboys began giving him a big ration of grief.

"And it's his trigger finger, too," one shouted. "We'll have to call him 'Shootless Jack' for a while." That was the highlight of the night.

The next morning, Stoney rode to Rita's place to talk with her about working as a deputy. Finished with her morning chores, she was at the woodstove cooking breakfast when he knocked on her screen door.

Seeing it was him, she shouted, "C'mon in, Stoney."

He removed his hat, opened the door and stepped in. "Smells mighty good, Rita."

"There's plenty enough for two," she offered.

"No thanks. Already ate."

"How 'bout coffee then?" she asked, fetching a clean cup from the shelf. "What's up?"

Blowing across the hot coffee, then gingerly taking a sip, he said, "I've got a favor to ask of you. And I'd like you to consider it real serious like."

"Okay... what is it?"

"I'd like you to be a part-time Deputy Sheriff."

As she swung her head to look at him, she dropped the fork she was using to turn the bacon. Then, looking back at the fork, she grabbed a rag, carefully retrieved it from the pan, and set it on the counter. Staring at the bacon, she finally said, "Deputy? Me... a woman?"

"Yup. You... a woman."

For a moment she was staring blankly, speechless. Then she asked, "One of Jake's mules kick you in the head this morning?"

Chuckling, he said, "No. Jake and Mack like the idea, too. In fact, it was Mack's suggestion."

She stepped slowly toward a chair, pulled it out and sat. She looked down at her hands. "Well, I'll be," was all she could think to say.

Stoney was letting her think on it, and heard a loud sizzling noise. "Rita... the bacon."

"Oh!" she exclaimed, and jumped to move the pan from the heat. Sitting back down, she said, "Well, I've always thought I could do a man's work... I guess I'm flattered. Just damn surprised is all."

"So, you'll take the job?"

"Sure I'll take it. You must think I can handle it, so I'll give it a try."

"Good. I'm glad," he told her. "Can you meet us at the hotel at noontime for some dinner?"

"I'll be there."

At dinner, Stoney showed her the new town ordinances. "The biggest thing I wanted to talk to you about, Rita, is that we're firemen trying to put out fires before they flare out of control. That means we don't get physical unless we have no other choice. And we don't fire a gun, except to protect someone."

"I understand," she said.

Stoney gave her a sly grin. "That means you have to control your ragin' reputation."

"I know... I understand," she repeated more seriously. "I can do it."

That afternoon we went about our business, monitoring the town in pairs — Stoney with Jake, and Rita with me. By suppertime, there'd been no disturbance of the peace. Most of the cowhands spent the afternoon taking baths in the bathhouse that Pat has at the back of his hotel. Baths were fifteen cents, and well worth it to a sweat-stained, dust-caked trail hand. Then most got a shave and a haircut. They kept Myron jumpin' for three hours straight.

Feeling fresh and clean all over, many visited the Mercantile to buy a new shirt, new Levi's, and some new underwear. Now they were ready for a big steak at the hotel diner. Rita and I took our turn for supper, eating at the hotel rather than Kristine's, to keep watch over the town guests.

Later many of the local ranch hands — done with their day's work and their supper — began drifting into town. The noise level was growing in both saloons. Nearing sunset, the four of us sat on the edge of the boardwalk between the saloons. Commenting on how calm things had been, Jake nodded down the street, asking, "Who are those four?"

Four riders were approaching the hitching rail beyond Dusty's. Studying them, Stoney said, "No idea. Probably best we keep a good eye on 'em though.

Nearing midnight, we hadn't had more than some loud shouting matches, and a few disgruntled cowhands upset over poker losses. Rita and I were in the hotel saloon making sure nothing flared up beyond that. Suddenly, Kenny Page came running through the swinging doors of the saloon. Staring down, and pointing in the direction of Dusty's, he said, "Trouble."

I glanced over at Rita, and the two of us took off running. Kenny was following close behind. When we reached Dusty's, I looked over the top of the doors trying to see what was happening. I could see Stoney, rifle aimed at one of the four riders we'd seen earlier, but I couldn't see Jake anywhere. Rita and I stepped in, spreading out on either side of Stoney.

I waited for a lull in the noise, then asked, "What's up, Sheriff?"

Without taking his eyes off his target, he said, "This fella here didn't bother to read our ordinances, I suspect, and drew his gun on Brock over there." Brock was the lippy cowhand at their arrival last night.

"Evidently, he took offense to Brock calling him a cheat. Figured he'd settle things hisse'f. I'm tryin' to help him understand it doesn't work that way anymore in Eagle Bluff."

I looked around the room thinking, *Any way you cut it, this could be real trouble.* I spotted two more of the riders across the saloon. One was particularly edgy, with a twitchy trigger finger. I kept close watch on him, like a bobcat watchin' a rattler. *Could be, all hell was about to bust a cinch.*

Seeing his target was getting a little more agitated, Stoney told him, "I've already got half pressure on the trigger of this here rifle. Do anything foolish, make any movement sudden like, and it'll rip you open. If you've any desire to taste bacon for breakfast ever again, lay your holster and gun on that table very carefully." Doing as Stoney had told him, things seem to be coming under control. I breathed a little easier.

Then Rita noticed movement near the second-floor railing. Dusty has rental rooms up there, and one of the four riders peeked around the corner. Seeing a rifle aimed at his partner, he drew and aimed at the Sheriff. "Stoney!" she shouted, as she swung her rifle and fired. She hit the gunman in the chest, spinning him to the balcony floor, as his gun fell to the main floor.

I quickly looked back to the edgy one, but too late. His gun cleared leather, and he fired just as I drew mine. He hit Rita in the upper chest, toppling her over a table to the floor. I fired, and hit him hard in the shoulder. It shattered bone, and spun him to the floor screaming and clutching at his shoulder.

Stoney covered the other two, who had raised their hands shouting, "Don't shoot... don't shoot!"

Jake, who had gone to use the outhouse, hurried in the back door just as I knelt by Rita. Shocked, he asked, "Is she all right?" I could tell that she was breathing, then heard a low groan as I carefully tried to turn her.

I looked at Kenny, and calmly asked, "Can you run to get Doc Undahl?"

"Yes... run," he said nervously.

"Go," I said, louder.

He turned, and left on a run. In what seemed like a long while, but actually wasn't more than a few minutes, Kenny came back, rushing through the swinging doors holding Doc's hand, tugging her through the doors. As she hurried over to where Rita lay, she must have noticed the puzzled look on my face.

"I was hurrying as fast as I could," she said, "but not fast enough for Kenny. So he grabbed my hand to help." She knelt by Rita, who was groggy but conscious, and began to examine her. Opening a couple buttons of Rita's shirt, she pulled the collar to the side. After checking the bullet wound, she gently turned her enough to cut the back of her shirt with a scissor. Pulling it open, she examined the exit wound.

"Well, at least it's a good wound, if there can be such a thing," she said. "It was clean in and clean out, without hitting anything vital. She hasn't had a huge blood loss either. She'll make it fine. A few weeks of painful healing, but she'll be fine."

"Good," I whispered. Then Jake, who had knelt near us, said the same, with a tender smile on his face.

"I'll need someone to fetch my stretcher, then help move her back to my place," Doc said. Several of the local ranch hands offered their help.

Next, she moved to the one who'd shot Rita. After checking him, she said, "He'll likely have a bum shoulder the rest of his life. Healthy enough to be shipped off to prison, though."

Then she went to the upper hallway to see about the fella who'd drawn on Stoney. She found him curled up, and in a lot tougher shape. "He's got some shattered ribs, but worse, he's lost a lung and a lot of blood. It'll be a lot more risky for this one."

"He can get an extended stay in the prison hospital," Stoney said matter-of-factly. Then moving back to Rita's side, he whispered, "Rita?"

Her eyes opened, and she whispered, "Yeah?"

"Thanks," he said, taking her hand in his.

"For what?" she asked, softly.

"For saving my life," he told her, more strongly.

"Just doin' my job, Sheriff." She tried to smile, but winced from the pain.

We locked up the other two gunmen and, after some questioning, concluded they were highwaymen types. They followed cattle drives lookin' for easy money from the cowpunchers at the poker table — or hard money, taking it from them in the deep shadows of the night.

Surprisingly, the cattlemen appreciated what we had done, and the price Rita had paid. They gave us *almost* no trouble the rest of their stay.

Monday, as I headed out early for the Witten's ranch, I saw a huge dust cloud that was lit by the morning sun's first rays. The cattle drive was on the move, bound for Colorado.

Chapter Twenty-Seven

Scarface sat in the shade of his porch roof, his feet resting on the rail. He was cleaning his rifles. He had a Sharps Model 1874, and a Winchester Model 1873. Cleaning them was his favorite form of relaxation. The Winchester was considered accurate to a hundred-fifty yards. With his, he'd shattered a gallon jug two hundred yards from his porch. The Sharps was accurate for a longer range, sometimes out to three hundred yards. He'd shot a bucket off the top of a fence post nearly four hundred yards away. Not many were as good.

As he cleaned the guns, he watched for the visitor he was expecting. He liked being out here alone, away from towns and people. His gaze scanned the far and lonesome land, running wild and free to the horizon and beyond. Wild and free like himself.

Here, ten miles from the closest neighbor, his shack sat on a knoll, and was sheltered by a stand of pinyon and juniper. From this knoll, he could see two miles in all directions, so had little concern for surprise visits. This visitor was expected to be here at one o'clock, and it was not yet twelve-thirty.

His was a one-room shack, with a corral on the north side to house his white mustang. He'd bought the mustang from a trader in northern Nevada. It was a strong horse that, like most of its breed, possessed great endurance. If pushed, it'd go until it collapsed, rather than ease up to rest. The other reason Scarface wanted a mustang, is that they're better than most watchdogs for alerting you when someone or something is near.

The original builder of the shack had chosen an ideal location. It has clear views in all directions and yet, sitting in the stand of trees, it isn't easily spotted against the skyline by anyone passing by.

And, if ever needed, there is a quick escape route. On the northeast side, a short way from the corral gate, is the mouth of a mesquite lined ravine that leads down to a long, winding canyon. If you don't know where the trail is located to get up and out of the canyon, your only choice is to retreat to where you had entered. Few whites travel this wilderness area, and very few know where to find the trail out of the canyon.

The Washoe, Paiute, and Shoshoni Indians, who'd lived in the area for hundreds of years, knew and still used the trail. Some said the Washoe had carved the trail into the canyon's sloped rocky sidewall more than a century ago. Only Scarface, and maybe a handful of other whites, knew of the trail and its location.

He had great respect for the Indians, and envied their understanding of nature, and ability to feel it, hear it, be a part of it. For many centuries they have believed the earth is their mother, and that all things — earth, water, air — are alive and speak to us. If we listen and watch, all things have something to tell us.

Above all, he respected their strength and bravery. Through the ages it had been a necessary attribute for their survival. Indians have great respect for courage in others. And they despise cowardice. If they see strength and bravery in an adversary, they may let him live to fight another day. If they sense fear and cowardice, they will kill without thought. Whites know very little of this kind of honor and bravery.

136

The most recent owner of this property was a loner named Wilson "Sniffy" Mayweather. The nickname "Sniffy" came from his habit of using dry snuff for nose sniffing. He had spent a couple of years living with relatives in England, and picked up the use there. When he returned to the Eagle Bluff area, he arranged for Roger Slenz, owner of the Mercantile, to have his brand of dry snuff shipped from England several times each year. Sniffy would pick it up on his occasional trips to town for supplies.

Roger, a stout man with a wonderful sense of humor, had also spent time in Europe. He enjoyed Sniffy's rare visits, talking mostly of their days in England.

Scarface recently met Sniffy, and visited him often. Envying his setting on the knoll, in the middle of three thousand acres, Scarface offered to buy it. He repeatedly asked him to sell, and Sniffy just as persistently told him no, he wasn't interested in selling.

Scarface finally offered an outrageously high price, and when Sniffy, who was amazed by the amount of the offer, still said no, Scarface drew his gun and shot him.

After burying him on the knoll, near the edge of the junipers, Scarface forged a bill of sale at a fraction of the price he had offered. In the "agreement," Scarface received ownership of the property, while Sniffy received cash, and assurance that he be buried on the knoll. To explain their agreement, Scarface contrived a story of Sniffy's poor health, and his desire to sell the property before it was too late. Then, in a matter of days, Sniffy was dead. His burial site is marked with a wooden cross. To show his unwavering loyalty, Scarface placed all of Sniffy's cash, and personal items, in a box that sits on a shelf in the corner of the shack, waiting for a relative to claim it.

Scarface glanced up, raised a hand to shade the bright midday sun, then focused sharply. Against the blue-white horizon he saw a dust cloud, likely that of a lone rider. He finished his gun cleaning, then hung the rifles on the wall in the shack. Returning to his rocker on the porch, he got comfortable to watch and wait. About twenty minutes later, the rider came up the slope of the knoll, and said, "Howdy, pod'ner." He eased his horse to a stop in the shade of some nearby pinyon.

Scarface said, "Hello, Warden," in a tone that was less than welcoming.

Sliding from the saddle, the Warden dropped the reins to ground hitch his horse where it stood. His was a well-trained horse, and reins on the ground anchored him as well as wrapping them around a hitching rail. He removed his hat, scanned the area, then reached for his bandana. After wiping his forehead, and the inside of his hat, he stepped onto the porch.

Scarface waved a thumb toward the door saying, "Grab a chair from inside."

Unimpressed with his partner's hospitality, Fitz came out with a chair, and asked, "Got anything cool to drink?"

"Only the spring water over there," Scarface gruffed, pointing to a nearby rocky slope. "You know where it is. The pail and dipper are on the counter."

Walking to the spring, pail and dipper in hand, Fitz tried to console himself about Mick's unfriendliness, lack of hospitality, and outright rudeness. Scarface's name is Michael O'Conner, and he goes by Mick.

After all, he thought, *I'm not dealing with him because I want his friendship. It's strictly business. So, to blazes with his lousy attitude and unfriendliness.*

He took several long, refreshing drinks of the water, and recalled how cool and clean it was. It flowed from the slope, and filled a small, natural pool formed in the rocks. The steady overflow streamed down to a small pond that lies well down the slope. Filling the bucket, he headed back to the porch, and his rude host. Settling into his chair, he waited a long while for Scarface to finally speak.

"Your message sounded urgent," Mick said.

"It is," Fitz replied. "I don't know if you've seen the new deputy in Eagle Bluff...."

"Is he the one who's also working out at the Witten place?" Scarface interrupted. He was staring at a large, soaring turkey buzzard.

"I think that's the same guy. Anyway, he made a visit to my office last week, asking all kinds of questions about the Kennedys, and about Connor Kennedy. I think it's time he goes, before he figures out our involvement in this whole thing."

Silence again, as Scarface continued watching the buzzard soar, wondering what it saw that might be dead and looking appetizing down below. Still staring up, he said, "I can arrange an accident... or worse."

"Better soon, as late," Fitz added.

"I'll take care of it," Scarface said, agitated.

"When are we gonna move on the gold?" the Warden asked, nervously.

"Soon... I'll let you know. Don't get fidgety."

"Alright, alright," Fitz said. "But I'll be a whole lot less fidgety with that nosy deputy out of the way."

They sat in silence, again, then Fitz finally said, "Well, I'll be gettin' back to Carson City. I'd like to make it before nightfall."

"Ride safe, Warden," Scarface said, not getting up or even glancing his direction. Evidently, the buzzard held Scarface's interest more than the Warden.

Chapter Twenty-Eight

Monday, Stumpy and I spent a long day ridin' the line, checking nearly thirteen miles of fence. Most of the repairs were minor, with only one seriously damaged piece. From the nearby tracks, it looked like an elk had tangled with the fence. In its thrashing about, it broke all but the bottom strand of wire, and snapped off one post, leaving a tangled mess.

In the far northwest corner of the ranch, we were reinforcing a corner post, by wiring a large stone to it to help anchor it in place. As we finished, I stood to stretch my back, then removed my hat, and wiped my forehead with my bandana. I wiped the inside of my hat and put it back on. With the brim shading my eyes, I soon noticed movement along a high ridge to the north of us. *Scarface again*, I thought.

"Hey Stump."

"Yeah?"

"I think that's our friend up there on that ridge. Make like you're still workin' on that post, while I get my glass, and check him out."

"You got it," he said, and began hammering the post. With my glass, I spotted the Mustang, then Scarface came into focus. Standing on the far side of his horse, he leaned over the saddle, and raised a spyglass to his eye. I pulled my glass down, and turned away before he could focus on me. For whatever reason, I didn't want him to know we were watching him.

"That's him, alright," I told Stumpy. "And he's got a glass on us."

"I'd sure like to know what he's up to," Stumpy said, throwing his hammer in the back of the wagon. For the next couple of hours, we caught glimpses of him, as he lingered in the distant shadows.

We got back to the ranch shortly after seven. Julie, knowing we'd be late, delayed supper, and watched for us through the window. Seeing us riding up, she stepped to the porch and called out, "Supper at seven-thirty boys." Stumpy waved to let her know we'd heard.

He turned to me, saying, "I'm so hungry I could eat a mule all by m'sef."

I laughed, saying, "Make mine a tender, juicy beef steak instead."

He grinned. "That does sound a mite bit tastier."

We took a while at the well pump, splashing off the day's dust, then joined them in the house. As we began passing food, Will asked about the condition of the fence lines.

"We're in good shape," Stumpy told him, as he reached for a biscuit. "Some minor repairs, and one hole that we fixed. It looked like a big elk had tried to square dance with the fence."

"Nice to know things are in good shape," Will said. Then he paused, and looked at me. "So I don't forget, you got an invite from the Kennedys."

"Really," I said. "Invite to what?"

"To supper at Brendan's place... tomorrow night at seven o'clock."

"Really," I said, again.

"Patrick came by earlier. Said he was headed home from visiting with his folks, and stopped to pass on their invitation."

"Good! I had mentioned to Pat that I was interested in meeting with his father," I explained. "So, he must've told him."

"What're you hoping for?" Julie asked.

"Hear his version of things. So far, he's the main character in this drama. I'd like to hear his story and, hopefully, get a sense of how truthful and forthright he is about it."

The next evening I rode up to Brendan's ranch at ten minutes of seven. It was a large, very nice home, with a big barn, and two other out-buildings. There were several horses tied to their hitching rail, and I recognized Patrick's dappled gray, with his finely tooled saddle. *Must be sittin' down with the whole family*, I thought.

I had Patch lie on the porch, then tapped on their door. Brendan answered, inviting me in with a smile and a wave. Introducing himself, he said, "Nice to finally meet you, Mr. MacAlan."

"Please, call me Mack."

"Only if you'll call me Brendan," he said.

"Agreed."

He was a man of medium height, probably five-eight, with strength evident on his sturdy frame. He had short reddish-brown hair, and a feel of self-confidence. He turned with a flourish to introduce Kate, his lovely wife.

"Very happy to meet you," she said pleasantly. I could hear a soft Irish lilt in her voice.

"My pleasure," I said, shaking her hand. She was a short, graceful woman. Her hair was long and wavy, and the auburn color highlighted her fair skin. One could imagine her to have been exceptionally attractive in her younger years.

"Come in. Sit down," she said. "Would you like a cup of coffee, or tea, before we sit for supper?"

Brendan said, "We don't drink much alcohol, but I have some very fine brandy if you'd rather that."

I hesitated a moment, then answered. "Tea sounds very good. I haven't had any in some time."

Brendan raised his finger and nodded, indicating he'd like the same. "Be right back with them," she said, turning toward the kitchen.

Just then, their three sons came from the kitchen to say hello. Brendan rose to his feet, and I did likewise.

"Mack, this is our oldest son, Adam. Adam... Troy MacAlan."

"Hello, Adam," I said, extending my hand to him. He resembled his father, with the same reddish-brown hair and stocky build.

"Glad to meet you, Mack," he said, with a strong handshake.

"This is our youngest son, Sean," Brandon said, holding a hand out toward the next son.

Sean stood eye-to-eye with me at six feet, and had a lean, but strong build. He, too, had a firm handshake, and said, "Hello, Mack." He had his mother's good looks and wavy auburn hair.

"Sean," I responded, nodding to him. Then I glanced back and forth between Sean and Adam, trying to see any resemblance.

"And you already know our son Patrick," Brandon said, patting him on the back. Pat stepped past his father to shake my hand.

"Yes, I do know him. And thanks, Pat, for arranging this get-together."

Kate came back carrying a tray with three cups of tea. "Sit... sit," she told us, lowering the tray to a nearby table. "You boys were already working on a cup of coffee, so I didn't fix you tea." The three of them retrieved their coffee, and joined us in the parlor.

After small talk about my working at the Witten ranch, and serving as Deputy Sheriff, Brendan said, "Patrick tells us that you're a straight shooter — both with your gun, and with your word."

I paused, feeling a little flush in my face. "I try to use both sparingly," I said, and a smile of appreciation showed in his eyes.

I brought up the troubles of the neighboring ranchers for the past year, and it wasn't difficult for him to sense what I was getting at. He looked at me for a long moment, then said, "The only thing that our family takes responsibility for is Connor shooting Wally Jacoby. For that, he went to prison and died. You know that painful story already."

"Unfortunately..." I said. "Had to be very hard losing a son, no matter the situation."

"Yes... it is," Kate said, with a heavy sadness. Then she brightened, and told us, "I think our supper is ready. Let's continue this at the dining table."

Their dining room was remarkably elegant for a ranch home in this western wilderness country. I guessed that the large, beautiful dining table and chairs had come from Europe. There was a large, impressively made hutch that held lots of delicate plates, cups, and other glass items that might have come from Ireland.

"You have such a unique and lovely home, Kate," I said, as I took my seat.

"Thank you," she said with a sweet smile. "We always dreamed of a home such as this... when we were still in Ireland. Brandon and I are from very poor, hard workin' families. Comin' to America was all we strived for. Now, since finding success, and some wealth, we regularly send money to our families back home, helping them have a little better life there. And we enjoy some of the finer things here as well."

146

I sensed a sincere modesty in what she said. She began serving our meal, which was as impressive as their dining room. She served a baked ham, mashed potatoes, sweet potatoes, vegetables from her garden, and freshly baked bread. The room was quiet, save for the clinking of forks and knives against fine china.

We enjoyed our food, and continued our conversation. In time, Brendan sat up straight, let out a big sigh, and gently pushed his plate away. "Don't think me stomach will accept another bite."

"I need to quit, too," I said. "I'm stuffed, but keep on eating just because it tastes so good." I slid my plate away.

"Well, let me clear the table then, while you men are visitin'," Kate said, rising from her chair. Her sons rose to help her.

Brendan looked at me with a seriousness. "As I've mentioned before, outside our responsibility for Connor's actions, we're as puzzled as all the rest about the things that've happened. Still, for fair reason I suppose, the fingers and rumors point in our direction."

Kate waited until he had finished, then asked, "Can I bring anyone fresh coffee, and a slice of apple pie?"

Brendan rubbed his stomach, saying, "Make it the tiniest of slices, luv." Then the rest of us agreed to a tiny slice, too.

Adam and Sean rose to help their mother carry them. Patrick said, "If you remember our conversation a while back, I mentioned the difficulty of proving our innocence, made more difficult by not being well liked."

"I take full blame for that," Brendan interjected. "My nature as a stern businessman has generally rubbed folks, leaving me with very few good friends. It's something I know about myself, and never had much luck trying to do things differently. Fortunately, our sons are a little better at being friendly. Probably get it from their wonderful mother." She set his coffee and pie in front of him, then leaned to kiss him on the forehead.

"As for Connor..." he continued, "I've never quite understood, nor figured that one out. I've come to believe in the notion that there is such a thing as a bad seed."

I turned my head, saying, "Thanks," as Sean slid pie and coffee in front of me. As they all sat once again, I asked, "Do any of you know about the rider on the white mustang?"

Adam answered, saying, "No, not other than the talk around the area. I even heard one ranch hand call him the 'Ghost Rider,' since he seems to come and go without a trace."

"Does seem a bit strange," Brendan added.

After more conversation, Brendan looked me in the eye for a long moment, then said, "You haven't known me, so you only have what I say. I mentioned earlier how you've built a good reputation as a straight shooter. Well... I honor my word above all else. I'm telling you that our family is not behind these troubles. I'll leave it to your instincts as to what you believe."

Chapter Twenty-Nine

After my visit, one that was much more enjoyable than expected, Patch, Blaze, and I were on the trail east toward the Witten ranch. I eased my weight back against the cantle, and relaxed in the saddle, pondering the Kennedy family. Thinking back to one of Brendan's last comments, my instincts told me they were decent, honest people, whose word you could trust.

As far as the dislike that many of the locals have for them... who knows? Brendan was likely right that it began with his stern, matter-of-fact nature as a businessman. Add to that the natural envy and jealousy people can cultivate toward those who have some success and wealth. Now stir the kettle with a trouble-making, hateful son... not surprising results.

"You know what Patch," I said, and saw his ears flick. "I don't think the Kennedys are behind any of the trouble that's been going on. I just can't see it from the kind of people they are." I leaned forward, patted the sides of Blaze's neck, then rubbed her ears. "So... where does that leave us?" They were both quiet and calm. Probably just as puzzled about the whole mess as I was.

The night was dark and silent. From horizon to horizon, countless stars sparkled like diamonds on black velvet. The quiet was pierced by the yelp of a coyote calling to a mate. A soft breeze rustled the leaves, playing a soft, sweet melody. The only other sound I heard was the soft, steady clop of Blaze's hooves. I was nearly lulled to sleep by the rhythm, as I sat comfortably in the saddle swaying with her motion.

After a time, I could hear something out ahead of us. I slowed Blaze and leaned forward, listening more closely. "What's that sound?" I whispered. Her ears pricked, and Patch's head raised.

They weren't sure either.

I urged Blaze into a cantor, straining hard to listen. Finally hearing it louder, I recognized the sound, and said, "That's a harmonica we hear. Someone else is traveling this trail tonight."

Soon, I could tell we were gaining on whoever it was, as the harmonica music grew louder and louder. When we crested a rise, I could see the outline of a wagon rolling down the trail.

We closed within thirty or forty yards, and the harmonica music continued. I slowed Blaze again, saying, "I don't think they hear us coming." I decided to call out to them, hoping we wouldn't scare the bejeebers out of 'em. "Hey, in the wagon," I shouted.

The harmonica went silent, and I saw the silhouette of a man's head appear around the side of the wagon. Then I heard, "Who we got back there?"

"Just a friendly stranger."

"Come on ahead, friend."

A bright moon had climbed above the horizon and, as we came alongside the wagon, I could see large red letters that advertised, "Dr. Michael Schlensick's Magic Elixir." Nearing the driver, I eased Blaze to a walk, then said, "Hello there."

"Howdy," he said, smiling and thumbing his hat. "I'm Mike... Mike Schlensick, like it says on the wagon."

"Pleased to meet you, Mike. I'm Troy MacAlan. Folks call me Mack."

"What has you on the trail this late, Mack?"

"On my way back from a visit. And you?"

"Workin' my way to Eagle Bluff," he said. "Hoping to sell some of my healing potions to the fine people there. How far do you think it is to town?"

"An hour 'n a half... maybe two."

"Well Mack, if you'd like, tie your horse to the wagon and climb aboard. I haven't had company for a few days."

He stopped his wagon, and I tied Blaze to the back. Climbing aboard next to him, I could see he was medium height, with a thick frame, a large barrel chest, and broad shoulders. His thinning hair was cropped short. He had a thin scar that ran from his hairline, across his forehead, then through his eyebrow. It stopped just short of the eyelid on his right eye.

He noticed my look at the scar, and said, "Had a guy come at me with a knife."

"How'd that work out," I asked.

"I ended up burying it in his chest, so that didn't work out so well for him."

"Came mighty close to losing an eye," I said.

"Yup. Always been glad it wasn't any closer." He tapped his mule with the reins. "Let's go Sarah Jane."

"Sarah Jane," I repeated. "Quite a name for a mule."

"Bit of a story behind that."

"I got some listenin' time," I said with a smile.

He grinned. "This mule I just always called 'Mule.' Sarah Jane was my sweet, lovely wife, and I lost her to heart failure a couple years back. She was sweet as sweet could be, but she had a little stubborn streak in her, too. Now and again, she was a bit like Mule... sweet, but stubborn as can be, too.

"Well, after I'd lost her, I decided to call Mule by her name. That way 'Sarah Jane' would be on my lips, and in my thoughts many times every day."

"Seems like you've got a bit of a sweet streak yerse'f," I said.

"Now, don't go spreadin' rumors like that, Mack."

I grinned. "Okay. I won't."

We rolled along in silence for a while, then he asked, "So, what do you do in Eagle Bluff?"

"I work for the Witten ranch, three miles this side of town. Sometimes as Deputy Sheriff in town, too." Changing the subject, I said, "I don't know where you planned to stay for the night, but you're sure welcome to park at the Witten place. Then you can head on into town in the morning."

152

"I just might take you up on that, if you're sure they wouldn't mind."

The next morning I awoke early, pulled back the curtain on our window, and looked to see if there was movement in the ranch house. I noticed smoke beginning to roll from the kitchen's chimney, and figured Julie was likely gettin' ready to cook some breakfast.

She's a wonderful cook, and I couldn't remember when I'd eaten better. Luckily, they'd been having just enough work to cover my room and meals, and leave me a few extra dollars for pocket money.

I walked to the house, tapped on the door, then stepped in and said, "Mornin', all."

"G'mornin'," Will replied, not looking up from the papers he was focused on.

Julie looked up from the stove. "Good mornin', Mack. How'd things go at the Kennedy's?"

"Actually... it went pretty darn good. How 'bout I wait 'till breakfast to tell you all about it."

"Okay," she said, stoking the kitchen stove. "I'll be starting it soon. Is Stumpy up-n-at-em yet?"

"Yup. He was sittin' on the edge of his bunk when I walked over here. I wanted to explain to you about the wagon parked near the barn."

"The snake oil peddler?" Will asked, still not looking up from his paperwork.

"Yeah. I ran into him on the trail last night, and told him he could park here for the night. Hope that's alright."

He set his pencil down, and looked up. "No problem at all. I think we met this one a couple years back. Seemed like a decent sort."

"I thought so, too. Glad you're okay with it."

Julie, who had started whipping some pancake batter, said, "Why don't you invite him to breakfast with us, Mack. We'll eat in a half hour."

Saying, "I don't know how he could pass on that," I turned, and hiked to his wagon. I tapped on the side door and, from under the wagon, heard, "Mornin'."

I crouched, and saw him crawl out from his bed roll. "Mornin' Mike," I said. "Didn't even notice you under there."

He moved out from under the wagon, raised up to his feet, and groaned, "Nnnn, nnn, nnn." Then he stretched, took a deep breath, and blew it out. "On nicer nights I generally sleep underneath. Cold or wet nights you'll find me inside."

"I came to give you Julie's invitation for breakfast."

Surprised, he said, "That sounds mighty good. I hate scroungin' up my own breakfast anyway."

"We'll eat in a half hour," I said, and went to feed Blaze and Patch. A while later, we walked in the kitchen, and I introduced Mike to everyone. Julie served delicious bacon and eggs, with hot cakes and syrup.

154

"So..." Stumpy started, then took another bite of bacon. "So, how did you get in the snake oil business?"

"Stump... that's a little rude," Julie scolded.

"No, that's fine," Mike said. "That's what most folks think of this profession. As a matter of fact, many are just that... snake oil hustlers. There are a few of us though, that have honest-to-goodness healing remedies."

"So, how did you get into it?" Stumpy repeated.

"It started with medical school out east. Then I was a family doctor, practicing over near St. Louis. I had always been interested in the use of herbs for healing... much like an Indian medicine man uses. For instance, dill oil soothes an upset stomach; white willow bark gives pain relief, and can be used in soap to eliminate dandruff; dandelion aids digestion. There are dozens of such remedies. And as far as the snake oil, it gets picked on unfairly. The oil from a particular snake is highly valued by the Chinese, and used a lot to treat joint pain.

"So, through the years, I've developed healing potions from natural herbs that seemed to help my patients. Of course, I had to stretch the truth a bit and say it was a prescribed medicine for their ailment. Otherwise, they'd start thinking 'snake oil.'"

"You think your stuff can cure people?" Stumpy asked, then sipped his coffee.

"I know that it can. Mack tells me you're occasionally troubled with some back spasms. One of my potions is a muscle relaxer and, I'm certain, would give you faster relief than anything you've been doing."

Stumpy set his coffee cup down, and looked at Mike. "Guess I should buy me some, if it'll work on my back."

"Tell you what," Mike said, as he wiped syrup from the corner of his mouth, "I'll give you one. In return, you promise to tell folks about it... if it helps you."

"Deal," Stump said, then raised his fork in salute of their agreement.

Changing the subject, Julie asked, "How about your visit at the Kennedy's, Mack?"

"Surprising," I said. "They're interesting people." I told them about the evening, and how likable I found them to be. "I think we can scratch them from the list of culprits."

"That's surprising," she said. "Not what I would have guessed."

"Me neither," Will added, slowly shaking his head. "So where does that leave us?"

"To my figurin', it leaves us with Warden Fitzig and Scarface as the most likely suspects."

He raised his eyebrows. "And how we gonna set our sights on them two?"

Chapter Thirty

After breakfast, Mike fetched a bottle of his muscle relaxing potion, and gave it to Stumpy. He thanked Julie for her delicious breakfast, then turned to shake Will's hand, saying, "Thanks for allowing me to be a guest at your fine ranch."

"You're welcome anytime, Mike."

Outside, I asked Mike how long he planned to be in Eagle Bluff? "Likely three or four days," he said. "It's another mighty big difference between me and the snake oil peddlers that breeze through. They're in and out of town in a day... before folks can figure out that what they sell is completely worthless. I like to stay a few days, and meet folks. Hopefully hear from some that my remedies are helping them."

"Maybe I'll see you in town before you move on then."

"I look forward to it, Mack."

That evening, Will caught me outside and talked to me about a new guitar he'd ordered for Julie's birthday. "It should be on the stage from Salt Lake City tomorrow. Do you think you could pick it up for me, then sneak it into the bunkhouse, and keep it there until next week? I don't want her to know about it, obviously, and don't want to try and explain a big package."

"Sure could. I wanted to visit Stoney anyway, to tell him about the Kennedys. I can pick it up for you in the afternoon."

"Good," he said. "That'll save me a ride to town, and tryin' to explain why I was going."

"I didn't know she played the guitar."

"Yes, she does. She often played and sang for her school kids. Her old guitar was crushed when we moved her things here, and, though she never complained, I know she was heartbroken. So, she hasn't played for a while, and I wanted to surprise her with a new one."

The next day I rode into town, and stopped at Stoney's office in the late morning. "Got time to eat?" I asked him, as I stood in the door.

"Sure do. How 'bout we walk down to Kristine's?"

"Let's mosey." As we walked, I asked, "Did Mike get to town with his wagon?"

"Yeah, earlier this mornin'. Jake let him park in the shade of the livery, like he has a time or two before."

"Can he gather a crowd down there?"

"Sure can. He hangs a big bell from the corner of his wagon, and when he clangs that thing it can be heard all through town. Folks have come to know that it means the entertainment is about to begin."

"Entertainment?"

"Oh yeah. He puts on a whole show... tells jokes, plays a harmonica, plays a banjo and sings, even does some magic. It's really quite a show."

"I guess I never thought about that. I suppose you have to have a way to gather folks around."

"Yup. And they go to see the show even if they have no interest in his potions. He usually does a show after dinner, and again after supper. First show's tonight."

We took a seat in Kristine's, and Karlee Kay, our waitress, asked if we'd like coffee. As she fetched it, Kristine stopped to say hello.

"Hey Stoney, how're you this mornin'?"

"Just dandy, Kris. How 'bout you?"

"Been a hectic morning, but things are under control now. We've got everything ready to go for the noon lunch gang."

She turned to me, asking, "And you Mack? I haven't seen your friendly face for a few days."

"Couldn't be better, Kris. What's good today?"

"Oh man, you gotta try the beef brisket. It's yummy." Then she patted my shoulder, and said, "I'd better get back to the kitchen. Good to see you two"

As we ate brisket, every bit as good as Kristine had told us, I told Stoney about my visit with the Kennedys. "So, unless there's someone out in the shadows we don't know about, it leaves the Warden and Scarface as the only likely culprits."

"Well... we can narrow our bird-doggin' to those two varmints then. Hopefully, they'll make a slip."

159

When we were ready to leave, I told Stoney, "I'm gonna head over to the Overland Stage office. Gotta pick up a package for Will."

"Okay," he said. "I'm headed down to see Jake."

"Tell him hello for me," I said, and turned to cross the street toward the stage office. Just down the street, I noticed Kenny Page workin' at his daily project, and walked toward him to visit.

"Hi, Kenny," I said.

He stopped what he was doing and, not looking up from the end of his shovel, said, "Hi, Mack."

"Did you take a break to eat some dinner, Kenny?"

"Yes. Ate dinner."

"Okay. That's good. You're doin' a good job there."

"Yes. Good job," he said, then went back to loading his wagon.

I walked in the Overland Stage office, which also serves as the town Post Office. Paul was at the counter sorting letters and packages, and glanced up at me. "Hey, Mack. What can I do for ya?"

"Nothin' yet, Paul. I'm just hangin' around, waitin' on the stage from Salt Lake City."

He glanced at his pocket watch. "Should be here in about twenty minutes. I'm gettin' today's mail ready to go out."

On the far side of the office, I noticed a nice camera sitting on a tripod. As I moved to look at it, I pointed and asked, "This yours?"

He looked up, and a broad smile lit his face. "Yes, it is," he said proudly. "I've been interested in photography for some time now." He came around the counter, and walked over. "I'm going to open a portrait studio... wedding photographs, family portraits and such. We've never had that here."

I lightly touched the fine wood of the camera, saying, "Impressive... very impressive."

"One of the finest available today," he explained. "I'm hoping for a shipment today... some photo paper and supplies for processing that I ordered from a company called E.& H.T. Anthony."

"You're still going to be Postmaster, and agent for the Overland Express aren't 'cha?"

"Oh yeah. Actually they've each been kind of like part-time jobs, anyway. With the photography studio business added in, it'll give me full-time hours. Maybe even a little more."

"That's really great, Paul. That should be quite a business for you."

"I hope so," he said with a shrug. "I've been a big admirer of Mathew Brady. He was the best photographer of the Civil War. He took thousands of photographs during the war that are amazing. He's also photographed eighteen of our country's Presidents.

"I saw a display of his work in St. Louis a few years back. That's when I decided I wanted to do photography. I order every publication I can about photography, and every piece I can find about his work."

I was impressed with Paul's knowledge, and said, "Well, you sure been doin' your homework. I wish you only good fortune with your new business. It'll be a fine addition to this town."

I sat on the bench outside the post office reading a copy of the Gazette, and waiting for the stage. After a bit, I heard low rumble of pounding hooves, and looked east. In the distance I could see the fluid motion of six horses, followed by a coach, and a cloud of dust.

As they neared the edge of town, the driver leaned back on the reins, shouting to his leaders, swings and wheelers, "Whoa thar... whoa now." He drove a six-up team, hitched to a nine-passenger, heavy duty coach. The coach appeared nearly full with passengers.

As they passed Jake's, he had the team slowed to a walk, then pulled them to a stop in front of the stage office. Paul stepped out onto the boardwalk, glancing at his watch. He clicked the watch shut, and dropped it in his vest pocket. When the noise and dust had settled, he shouted, "Right on time, Smiley."

"Ain't nothin' but, with me in the box," Smiley snarled. He looped the reins on the box rail, then climbed down to stretch.

"You got any packages or mail for us on your load?" Paul asked him.

"Yup. Two packages up top, 'n one package and the mailbag tucked in the boot. I'll get 'em directly... soon as I take care of the folks." He reached to open the coach door for his passengers.

I got up from the bench, and walked over to stand next to Paul. I guess I was curious to see the passengers as they unloaded.

The first was a young girl, maybe eleven or twelve years old. Next was a slightly older, taller girl, maybe sixteen. Then a woman, who could've been their mother, gracefully stepped out. She reached up, removed her hat and shook out her hair. As she did, the sun caught the red tones of her beautiful auburn hair.

When she looked up, her striking green eyes locked onto mine. I froze, holding my breath. I couldn't seem to move until she finally glanced down at the boardwalk, ready to step onto it. I quickly stepped forward, reached out my hand, and said, "May I?"

"Yes, thank you," she said, and took my hand.

When her skin touched mine, a shiver ran through my arm, and I froze again, speechless. She stepped onto the boardwalk next to me, and said thank you, again. When I didn't respond, she slowly looked down at my hand, then smiled at me.

I glanced down. "Oh... I'm sorry!" I said, nervously, and slowly released her hand.

"Not at all," she said, with a tilt of her head and, once again, a soft smile.

The driver began unloading luggage from the back boot, setting it on the boardwalk. The last item he removed was a carton that read, "Will Witten, Eagle Bluff, Nevada". *Must be the guitar*, I thought.

Then the driver climbed up top, and began throwing down more luggage and packages, while Paul caught them and set them on the boardwalk.

When they were finished, the woman with glowing green eyes asked Paul, "Is there a nice hotel in town where we could stay?"

"Yes there is, ma'am. At the corner down there, on the right side," he said, pointing for her. "That's the Eagle Bluff Hotel. It's a fine place."

"Thank you, so much. I think we'll go have a look."

I glanced down at their luggage, and saw they had five bags for the three of them. "Excuse me," I said.

She turned my way with a friendly, "Yes?"

"I'm headed that direction. I'd gladly help with a couple of your bags."

She looked down at them, then back at me. "That would be mighty nice of you. Thank you."

"Glad to help," I said, grabbing the two largest bags.

Chapter Thirty-One

As we walked toward the hotel, I asked, "Are you staying in town long?"

"No, maybe a night or two, then my nieces and I are on to San Francisco to visit my brother and his family. We've been traveling for over a week now, and I told the girls we could take a break here for a couple days. Then it's back on a stage again."

"Well, you picked a good town. There's good people, and lots of nice sites in the area."

At the hotel, I set their bags near the registration desk. She shook my hand, and thanked me. It sent a sensation through me... again.

Then she said, "I hope I'm not being too forward, but if you're available for supper, I'd like you to join us. It would be very nice, and I'd really like to have you tell my nieces and me about your town, and this area. My main reason for bringing them on this trip, was to give them an experience of our great western frontier."

Momentarily tongue-tied, I finally said, "It'd be my pleasure to join you. How 'bout I meet you right here at five o'clock."

"That's just fine. We're going to try to nap this afternoon, so... see you here at five." She smiled, then quickly added, "Oh, by the way, my name is Geraldine Hall. Please call me Geri. These are my nieces, Jenna Lyn and Lauren."

"I'm Troy MacAlan. Friends call me Mack."

Jenna Lyn was a tall girl, maybe five-nine, and very attractive. She seemed shy, and smiled sweetly when I nodded to her. Lauren was cute and a little less shy, as she gave me a cheerful, "Hi!" with eyes that sparkled.

Geri was a petite woman, just over five feet tall, and exceptionally attractive. I nodded, and thumbed my hat again, saying, "See you at five."

I walked back to the stage office to check on Will's package. When I stepped in the door, Paul had a sly grin. He asked, questioningly, "I'm headed that direction?" Then he broke into laughter, adding, "Sure you were."

"Well... you know..." I mumbled, turning up my hands, and shrugging.

"Yes, I know. I, too, noticed how lovely she is."

Feeling a little flush in my face, I grinned and asked, "What about Will's package?"

"Right here," he said, bringing it out. "Anderberg Music Company? Do you know what it is?"

"It's a guitar for Julie. A surprise for her birthday next week." Then I whispered, "Shhhh, it's a secret."

"Shhhh... won't say a word," he said softly.

At five o'clock I was on the boardwalk about to go in the hotel, when I noticed Geri and the girls coming from the boardwalk across the street. I waved, saying, "Hi there, ladies."

166

Lauren was the first to answer, with a friendly, "Hi, Mack," as she showed a big grin.

Jenna Lyn just smiled her sweet smile.

Geri waved, saying, "Hello, Mack." Then she stepped onto the boardwalk, and said, "We've been out strolling, and looking the town over. We met Dr. Undahl, Ann, working in her front yard. A very nice lady. Probably an excellent doctor, too."

"Yes, to both," I said, nodding. "Are you ready to have some supper?"

"Let's eat!" she replied.

In the hotel diner, we ordered and, while we waited for our meals, I asked, "So, did you meet anyone else?"

"We met Big Jake," Lauren said, with bright eyes.

"And, wow, is he big!" Jenna Lyn added, with heavy emphasis on 'big.'

"He told us they have two daughters, roughly their ages," Geri said, pointing to her nieces. "They're excited to meet them."

I nodded. "I think you're right. Jake's one of the best, and his girls are very nice. I think you'd have lots of fun with them. You might learn a little of what it's like being a girl in this western frontier, too."

"Maybe we could spend the day with them tomorrow, Aunt Geri," Lauren said excitedly. "Maybe even go on a horseback ride."

"Maybe so," she told her. "We'll have to speak with Jake, and be sure it's okay with his family. What do you think, Jenna?"

"I think it'd be fun."

"Jake's oldest girl, Cambria, is close to your age Jenna. She's quite a horse lover. I'm sure she'll take you two for a ride."

Our waitress brought our supper, and I said to her, "Whitney, these ladies are visiting from Chicago. This is Geraldine... and Jenna Lyn... and Lauren. They're going to be visiting for a couple days."

"Are you originally from here, Whitney?" Geri asked.

"Yup. Born and raised here."

"And you like it, obviously."

"Yes, I do. I visited St. Louis once, and don't think I'd like big cities. I prefer it here. This is home. Things seem way too hectic in a big city."

We began eating, and I was trying to work up the courage to ask Geri a question. I started several times, but hesitated each time. Finally, I blurted out, "If the girls get a chance to spend the day with Jake's daughters, maybe you'd like to go for a buggy ride with me, and see some of the countryside."

"I'd like that," she said. I felt relieved and thrilled at the same time. Then I was hoping that Jake had a nice buggy I could use.

Now that I had my courage built up, and seemed to be doing okay, I said, "It's my turn to be a little too forward... are you married?"

She showed a soft smile, as she gazed out the window for a moment. Then she said, "Widowed. I was married eight years, then lost my husband."

"I'm sorry," I said, hesitantly.

"It's quite all right. John worked for the railroad, and was injured in a big accident. He didn't make it through. I lost him four years ago."

"And you never had children?"

"No, we didn't. That added to the loss. It's why I've been so close to Jenna and Lauren these last few years. We have lots of fun together, and I can treat them like my own. My sister doesn't mind a bit. She's very understanding, and is not a bit jealous."

"She's just like our second Mom," Lauren said.

Geri smiled, then reached over and held both Lauren and Jenna's hands for a moment. "You two are the best. My sister is very lucky."

We were quiet for a while, eating our supper, then Lauren said, "We met Mike, too. The snake oil salesman with the nice wagon."

I chuckled, and Geri said," Lauren, that's not polite to call him that."

"But that's what he said."

"He was only joking about folks calling him that. He's a trained medical doctor, and it sounds like he makes very good remedies."

"Well, anyway," Lauren continued, "we've gotta go watch his show after we're done eating."

"Yes, we will have to do that," Geri said, with a nod of her head, and a poke at Lauren's side, which made her jump and laugh.

Finished with our supper, we walked outside to the boardwalk. "Should we stroll toward Jake's?" I asked. "See when Mike is going to start his show?"

"Yeah! Let's go," Lauren said, tugging on Geri's arm.

"Here we go..." Geri joked.

We'd barely begun to walk, when we heard the loud clanging of a bell.

Chapter Thirty-Two

"There's his bell," Lauren said excitedly. "Mike said he rings a bell when the shows gonna start." She was out in front, and pulling away from us, so we picked up the pace, and walked faster towards Jake's.

The early evening sun cast long shadows across the street. Out on the open range, it lit the sage with a purple sheen. The high buttes and mountains glowed against a blue sky. Geri pointed in the distance beyond Jake's, and said, "How beautiful!"

As we neared, we could see there were a couple dozen folks gathered behind Mike's wagon. The back of the wagon was dropped down to make a platform, suspended by a heavy rope on each corner. A curtain hung across the wagon opening, making a nice stage backdrop. Mike was on the platform playing a harmonica.

"Let's try to get close," Lauren said, dodging past some of the gathered crowd.

Geri nudged me, saying, "If you don't mind, let's slip off to the side, and stand in the shade of that cottonwood. It'd be much more comfortable."

"Sounds good by me."

"I think I'll go over by Lauren," Jenna told us, then moved through the crowd.

"Probably doesn't want to be stuck with us adults," Geri whispered.

Mike was just finishing a tune called *Soldiers Joy,* and noticed us standing in the shade. As he slapped his harmonica against a white handkerchief, he called out, "Hello, Mack. Glad to see you could make it." Then, nodding toward Geri, he added, "And you too, ma'am. So happy to have you here."

I shouted back, "Hey Mike, thanks for reserving our space in the shade."

"Prime seats," he said, grinning. Looking over the crowd, he waved, saying, "Step a little closer folks. Don't be shy." Seeing more coming down the street, he began playing *Sweet Betsy from Pike,* to give them time to move closer. Finishing that tune, he cleaned his harmonica again, and dropped it in his pocket. Then he brought out his banjo, and pulled the strap over his head. Hitting each string with a pick, he turned the peg to tune it. Finally satisfied, he strummed a couple of chords, saying, "This is an old Chinese song... *Tu-Ning,*" which brought a few chuckles, and lots of groans.

"Who knows the words to *Oh Susannah?*" he asked. A lot of folks nodded, and a few raised their hand.

"Good! You folks sing along with me." He strummed a 'D' chord, or so he said, and started singing. He had a deep, baritone voice, and strong lungs. Even those hanging back in the distance could hear him. By the time he'd sung "... I come from Alabama wid my banjo on my knee," he had most of the crowd clapping the rhythm, and singing along with him.

"Great job!" he shouted, hanging his banjo on a hook. "We've got more good sing-along tunes coming up real soon, but first... Who'd like to win a quarter?"

172

Lots of hands shot up in the air, but Mike focused in on Jenna, who hadn't raised her hand. "How 'bout this young lady right here," he said, pointing to Jenna.

She glanced around to see who he was pointing at, then began to turn red, and asked, "Me?"

"Yup. You. There's nothing to it. Just come right on up." He moved to the side where a set of steps sat on the ground, then reached out his hand, saying, "Step right up here, miss. You could win a quarter."

With a friendly push from Lauren, Jenna reluctantly climbed the steps. Mike took her hand, and moved her to the middle of the platform. She briefly put her hands over her face, then, taking a deep breath, she lowered them and looked out over the crowd, as though deciding she could do this.

"Thanks for being so brave," Mike said. "It's not easy getting in front of a hostile crowd like this, is it?" She smiled and blushed, as most of the crowd laughed.

Mike lightly touched her shoulder to move her forward, saying, "Tell us your name."

"Jenna Lyn Johnson."

"Jenna Lyn... what a beautiful name. Are you from Eagle Bluff?"

"No, I'm from Chicago."

His eyes widened. "Chicago... Wow! That's a big city. What brings you way out here?"

"We're on our way to San Francisco to visit an uncle."

"Well, good for you. Are you liking it here?"

She gave a big nod. "Yeah. A lot!"

"Me, too," Mike said. "How would you like to win a quarter, Jenna?"

"Sure!"

Taking a shiny quarter from his vest pocket, he held it up for the crowd to see, saying, "All you have to do to win this shiny quarter, Jenna, is help me make this disappear, and then reappear again. It'll be a magnificent feat of prestidigitation...." He paused, looking from Jenna to the crowd, then back to Jenna again. "How'd you like that word?"

She grinned, saying, "Never heard of it."

"I'll bet most of these folks haven't heard of it either. Now Jenna, so no one thinks there's any shenanigans going on here," he pulled his pants pockets inside out, letting them hang in a comical look, as he turned completely around on the stage.

He stood there, holding his arms out to the side, and looking over the crowd. "As you can plainly see, my pockets are empty."

Then, staring down at a gentleman standing near the platform, he leaned over, and said, "Really, really empty friend. Could you loan me a couple bucks?" That brought some big laughs, especially from the gentleman he was speaking to.

He reached behind the curtain, and brought out a file. "I'm going to put a notch in this coin to identify it." He drew the edge of the file across the coin a couple of times, then asked, "Can you see the notch?"

"Yes, right there," she said, pointing.

Hesitating, he said, "Maybe we should put one more notch on it to be sure." He held the coin up, and touched the file to it. "What do you think? About this far apart, Jenna?"

"A little farther apart."

"Right here?"

"Right there!"

He grinned at the crowd, then filed a second notch. "There we have it." He put the file away, and held the quarter in his upturned left hand, between his thumb and forefinger for all to see.

"Now... I simply take the coin in my right hand...." He lowered his right hand, closing it around the coin, then held his fist out toward the crowd. He slowly opened his hand, exposing the coin. "See... nothing to it. Except, this time Jenna's going to make it disappear."

He paused, turning to smile at her, which caused her to blush again. "This time, when I grab hold of the coin in my right hand, I'd like you to take your hand, with its magical powers, and pass it over mine." He took a deep breath, looked out over the crowd, then asked, "Are you ready, Jenna?"

She held out her hand, and shrugged. "I guess so."

He held the coin up again in his left hand, and slowly closed his right hand around it. Then, with a flourish, he held his right fist out for all to see. "Now it's time for you to use those magical powers, Jenna."

Taking a step forward, she raised her hand and circled it over his outstretched fist. Mike slowly opened his fist, exposing an empty hand. A few in the crowd murmured their surprise.

"There you have it, ladies and gentlemen. Now comes the true test. Can she make it reappear?" He patted his out-turned pockets, then up and down his shirt sleeves. He held his hands out to the side, and shrugged, as though to say, *Nope, I don't have it.*

Looking at Jenna, he said, "Your pretty dress has two pockets at the waist. Could I very carefully look to see if the coin is in one?" With her approval, he reached, and gently pulled the closest pocket open. He glanced in it, then at the crowd, shaking his head no. He did the same with the other pocket, then turned to the crowd with a look of frustration. Then he patted his own clothes and pockets again.

"I'm sure you have the coin Jenna, but I don't want to do the searching. Would you check your hair, behind your ears, up your sleeves... everywhere."

She felt around her hair, her ears, and then her neck. She rubbed up and down her sleeves. "Nope."

"Maybe somewhere in your dress?" he urged.

She patted her shoulders, sleeves, down her sides, her pockets... then she froze. Her eyes grew wide, as she reached in her right pocket, and pulled out a quarter.

"Does it have two notches?" Mike asks.

"Yes," she said, laughing and holding it up for everyone in the audience to see.

"There you have it ladies and gentlemen!" he shouted. "Jenna the Magnificent." The crowd cheered and applauded, even those who knew how the trick was done.

Mike shook her hand and, as the crowd quieted, said, "That quarter is yours, to treasure all the days of your life... or spend tomorrow, it's up to you." Urging the crowd to applaud, he added, "Thank you, Jenna Lyn!" and helped her down the steps. Lauren hugged her sister excitedly, then asked to see the coin, and waved it high for us to see, too.

When the crowd quieted, Mike said, "Before I grab my banjo again, and get you to sing some songs with me, I want to ask you..." He paused, bringing out a bottle of brown liquid. He held it up, then slapped it with his hand. "Draw near friends... let me ask you....

"Are your feet sore? Do they sweat and have a strong, disagreeable odor?

"Does the perspiration beneath your arms have an ancient and long-distance smell? One that offends your loving mate?

"Is your breath so foul that it causes friends to keep their distance?" He was rattling on at a fast pace now.

"If you do friends, Dr. Mike's Magic Elixir will heal any soreness, and destroy any odor. By using my magic elixir, your friends will once again draw near, and your enemies will bless you.

"This amazing remedy," he said, slapping the bottle again and talking much louder, "will cure all ills. It heals all sprains, bruises, flesh wounds, cuts, burns, chilblains, ulcers, piles, sore feet, ankles, knees, hips, shoulders, necks, backs..."

He paused, took a deep, relaxing breath, then lowered the bottle. Looking around the audience, he finally smiled and said, "That's what you expect to hear from a typical 'Snake Oil Salesman' isn't it?"

He saw lots of nodding heads. "Well, folks, with me that's just part of the entertainment, not what I sell. I'm a medical doctor. I used to practice near St. Louis. I've developed a number of remedies and medications from natural plants and herbs. Some can ease sore muscles... calm upset stomachs... aid in digestion... cure cuts and burns... help any number of ailments.

"But, obviously, there's not one remedy for every ill, so I can't sell the same potion to all. And, I'm not trying to sell anything right now, only entertain you.

"I'll be in town for the next few days. If you stop to see me, tell me your ailment, I'll tell you if I have something that will help. And I will only recommend one of my potions if I believe it will truly help you.

"Meanwhile..." he turned, and reached for his banjo, "Let's have some more fun."

Chapter Thirty-Three

"Wasn't that great!" Lauren shouted, as Mike's show ended, and the girls came to stand with us in the shade. Jake and his wife, Sheryl, had joined us, while their daughters went to stand with Lauren and Jenna. It was easy to see the girls had gotten acquainted, and were having a good time together.

"That was fun!" I answered. "And, how 'bout your big sister, 'Jenna the Magnificent.'"

Jenna smiled, reached in her pocket, then held up her shiny new quarter.

"That's a few hour's wages for a lot of cowhands," I told her.

"Really?"

"Yup, really."

Sheryl said to Geri, "Cambria and Samantha are really excited to have Lauren and Jenna spend the day with them tomorrow. Can they come over in the morning, and join us for breakfast?"

"I think that would be great," Geri said, smiling at her excited nieces.

"Why don't you and Mack join us, too?"

Geri looked my way for a response. I shrugged, saying, "Sounds good to me."

"Me too," she agreed, then asked, "What time?"

"How about seven o'clock," Sheryl answered. Then she smiled at Jake, adding, "We don't have to eat so early tomorrow."

"Fine by me," Jake said.

I asked him if he had a horse and buggy that I could rent for tomorrow. "I'm going to take Geri for a tour of the area."

"I have a good one, nearly new, that you can *use*," he said, with heavy emphasis on use. "There'll be no rent," he added, sternly.

"Okay... okay," I said, laughing.

At breakfast the next morning, Cambria told her new friends, "You get to help with chores this morning, and see what life is really like for us out here. Later, we'll go for a long horseback ride. We can pack a lunch and have a picnic out on the range. Then we'll be back in plenty of time for evening chores."

Geri turned to Sheryl with a worried look. "Is that safe for them to do?

"Oh, sure it is. Cambria knows what she's doing, and will keep them safe."

"Okay," Geri said, still a little uneasy.

"We'll be fine, Aunt Geri," Jenna said, reassuringly. "I even think helping with the chores will be interesting, and kind of fun."

As we finished breakfast, Geri thanked them, and said to Sheryl, "I'd like your family to be our guests at the hotel diner for supper this evening."

"Nonsense," Sheryl said, in a friendly tone. "You'll come back here for supper."

"Okay," Geri agreed. "But only if you let me help. I'm pretty good in the kitchen."

"It's a deal," Sheryl said.

Outside Jake's barn, I hitched a horse named Santa Fe to the buggy. Offering my hand to Geri, I helped her get aboard. I thanked Jake, and steered the horse away from the barn onto Main Street. "We'll be back in time for supper," I shouted.

Pulling to a stop in front of the Post Office, I said, "I'm gonna grab the guitar I mentioned, the one Will Witten bought for Julie's birthday. We can drop it off at the ranch, and you can meet them. I'll be right back."

Inside, Paul raised his eyebrows as I walked in the door. "Taking the lovely lady for a ride are you?"

"Yes... I am... nosey."

"Guy's gotta keep up with all the goings-on, ya know."

"I know," I said, giving him a friendly smile. "Have you got Will's package?"

He was already moving to bring it out. "Here you go. Have a fine day." He glanced out the window toward Geri, then grinned.

Outside, I slid the carton into the buggy and climbed aboard. Taking the reins, I lightly tapped the horse, saying, "Git-up thar, Santa Fe."

"Santa Fe?" she asked.

"Yup. Don't know the reason behind it, but that's her name." She moved into a nice smooth trot, and we headed for the ranch. As we rolled along, I could see Geri's head slowly moving side to side, taking in all the sites. She seemed to be very comfortable.

Meanwhile, I was nervously trying to think of things to talk about, when she said, "Nevada is so beautiful. Chicago is a great city, but the Midwest is mostly flat prairie. Out here... the sage, the jutting rock formations, the high buttes and mountains... they're all so wonderful. And the colors so beautiful."

Seeing how much she was enjoying the ride, and the Nevada landscape, I finally relaxed and enjoyed it with her. As we neared the ranch, I could see Will and Stumpy working on the door of the barn. Will laid his hammer down, and waved to us. Stumpy gave a quick glance, looked back down at his work, then snapped his head back up again with a surprised look on his face.

As we pulled to a stop, Stumpy grinned, saying, "I figured you stayed in town another day for no particular reason. I can see I was all wrong."

Trying to ignore his comment, I said, "Geri, this is Aldus Ambrose Giles."

"Stumpy, ma'am, and I'm very pleased to make your acquaintance."

She shook his hand, saying, "As well, kind sir."

Then, interrupting Stumpy's grip on her hand, I said, "Geri, this is Will Witten."

"Pleasure meeting you," he said, thumbing his hat.

"The pleasure's mine," she said, nodding to him.

"I'm gonna get Julie's guitar hid away before she comes out," I said, climbing down from the buggy. Then I reached a hand toward Geri, asking, "Can I help you down?" She took my hand and stepped from the buggy, saying thank you.

"I'll be right back," I told them, grabbing the guitar, and hurrying toward the bunkhouse.

As I came back out, Julie was opening the screen door, and stepping onto the porch. "Hi, Mack," she shouted. "I see you have a friend with you."

"Yes, I do. Come on over and meet her."

I introduced them, and Julie asked if we had time for a cup coffee or tea. "I think we do," Geri answered, then glanced my direction.

"Sure we do. Make mine tea."

"Me, too," Geri added.

We sat visiting a while, and I told them we were going to tour the area a little. "I want to show Geri some of our beautiful countryside. And I've wanted to see some of the rugged area west and north of here myself."

"That's over into Shoshoni and Paiute territory," Will said. "But they've been friendly for quite a few years, so you shouldn't have any trouble."

"You won't be havin' no trouble," Stumpy said, shaking his head. "If you run across a Shoshoni who calls himself Cameahwait... named for his great-grandfather, it means 'He who never walks'... tell him howdy for me."

"A friend of yours?" I asked.

"Yup. Met him a few years ago."

"Tell them that story, Stump," Julie said.

He eased back in his chair, mulling over the story in his mind. He took another sip of coffee, then started. "This was back a couple years before I came to work here. I was huntin' deer early one mornin'. The folks I was stayin' with were plenty hard up, and we needed some meat, so I thought I'd do some hunting.

"Anyway, there's some good herds of mule deer up north of here, gettin' into the Shoshoni territory. I was up there at daybreak, ridin' slow, watchin' the sage and trees for any movement. Maybe catch a glint of morning sunlight shining off an antler.

"Well, I spotted a dandy. He was a big buck, with a wide rack, and lots of meat on his bones. Unfortunately, I spotted him at the very time he caught my scent. He was to his feet, bounding through the sage and up the slope before I raised my rifle. Where he was headed, took him around a knoll and into a small ravine. I figured I could circle left, and cut him off on the far side. He'd likely be watching t'other way, where he'd seen me.

184

"I tied my horse, and headed off on foot, hoping to get a shot before he spotted me again. I walked slow and quiet, on the lookout for movement. Finally, coming to where I should see him, I had a couple of surprises.

"First, I spotted a Shoshoni knelt and gutting a deer. *My deer*, I thought, a little angered. Then the Shoshoni noticed me, as I began to raise my rifle. He had a shocked look on his face, and he froze. He flinched when I fired a shot, and was startled when a mountain lion fell from the ledge above him. We've been mighty close friends ever since that day. So... you tell him hello for me, if you run across him."

"I'll do that, Stump. That's an amazing story." I drank the last of my tea, and asked Geri, "Ready to take a buggy ride?"

"I sure am." Rising from her chair, she thanked the Wittens for their hospitality. Turning to Stumpy, she said, "Be sure to visit if you're ever in Chicago."

He grimaced, then shook his head. "You'll more likely see me in a petticoat, as see me in Chicago."

SEAT JOCKEY

HORN

CANTLE

SEAT

CHEYENNE ROLL

FORK

BACK JOCKEY

LATIGO HOLDER

SKIRT

LATIGO

RIGGING DEE

RIGGING DEE

FENDER

SADDLE STRINGS

STIRRUP LEATHER

FLANK BILLET

STIRRUP

FLANK CINCH

FRONT CINCH

CONNECTING STRAP

Chapter Thirty-Four

Scarface decided it was time to hunt down this guy... Deputy MacAlan. Time to ease their worries. The Warden tended to be a nervous-nelly, but maybe he was right about this one.

The next morning, at daybreak, he headed from his shack on the knoll, and rode half a day to the Witten's. Scouting the lay of the land, he chose a high, rocky slope, south of the ranch. He climbed two-thirds up the slope, and found a good perch. Looking north, with the sun at his back, and the top of the rocks behind him keeping him in the shadows, he was well hidden, and had a wide view of the ranch. He sat comfortably on a flat rock, with a huge boulder for a backrest. Next to him, on another flat rock, he laid his spyglass, Sharps rifle, and canteen. He was set for the day.

He was amazingly patient when posting like this. He could sit quietly all day, seldom moving, and rarely needing to stand or stretch. His keen vision missed little. It was as though he became part of the landscape, watching and listening for the slightest movement or sound.

For the first two hours he saw nothing of interest. Then, far off to the west, he noticed cattle coming over a rise, herded by two cowhands. He slowly lifted his spyglass, and focused on the riders. The first he recognized as Will Witten, riding his handsome Sorrel. He moved the glass to the second, and thought, *That's that sawed-off cowhand... Stubby, or whatever the heck his name is.* They were cutting calves from the herd, and pushing them toward the barnyard. He was hopeful that MacAlan would be the next to come over the rise.

After nearly an hour, the two riders had moved their calves into a corral by the barn. A third rider never had appeared. Scarface leaned against the boulder and relaxed his vigil, taking a drink from his canteen. He caught a glimpse of movement, and looked to see a large hawk soaring silently above the sage, hungrily watching for its next meal.

Throughout that afternoon and evening, he'd seen nothing of MacAlan. As it got too dark to see beyond the rocky slope, he climbed down, and walked to the stand of trees where he had tied his mustang. He mounted up, and turned the horse toward Eagle Bluff.

A short way from town, there's a spot in the rocky terrain, where he'd sat watch over the town a few times before. He'd camp nearby, and at sunrise be in that perch, watching for MacAlan. Finding a spot to camp, he swung down and unsaddled the mustang. He drove a picket pin in the ground, and tethered the horse to it. He spread his ground sheet, stretched out on it and covered himself with a blanket. In no time, he was snoring.

He slept hard through the night, until the sound of birds stirred him. Opening his eyes, he could see the faint glow of early dawn. He yawned, rubbed his eyes and got up. Deciding the tiny meadow was secluded enough to leave the mustang, he moved the picket pin to an area of fresh grazing. After walking the mustang to a nearby pool, and letting him drink his fill, he tethered him to the pin for the day.

For breakfast, he ate jerked beef and drank from his canteen. More than once he'd gone a couple days on nothing but jerked beef and water. Climbing to his spot up the rocky slope, he sat waiting for the sun to light Eagle Bluff. As before, he laid out his spyglass, rifle and canteen. He was ready for another day of hunting.

From this perch, he could see down Main Street to the hotel at the corner. He couldn't see around the corner to the other side of town, but was certain if MacAlan was in town, he'd see him. With the hotel, post office, sheriff's office and livery in view, MacAlan was sure to walk this side of town, and he'd spot him.

Glancing over his shoulder, the eastern sky was turning a reddish-purple. In the growing light, he saw Jake open the doors to the livery, and light a lantern inside. Soon he could see bright coals glowing, as Jake stoked his forge. An enclosed wagon sat next to the livery. There was writing on the side, but with the angle the wagon sat, he couldn't quite make it out what it said. Something about magic elixir. *Likely some kind of peddler*, he thought.

The eastern sky was glowing with a brighter copper-red color now, and Eagle Bluff was coming to life. Soon, a few wagons and buggies rolled into town, and people were moving about, starting their day. He saw the preacher come down the boardwalk, then climb the church steps, prop the doors open, and open a few windows. *Probably to get some fresh air moving, and pray for a while*, he thought, disdainfully.

He noticed the sheriff come round the corner, and stop to visit with a group of folks in front of the hotel. Pat, one of the Kennedy brothers, was in the bunch, along with Paul, the postmaster, and Tom Bray, the banker. Soon, they each went their way to open their offices.

Still no sign of MacAlan.

He watched, and the early risers were on the move, going about their business. "Good citizens, all," he whispered, sarcastically.

189

Then, scanning around him, he caught sight of a golden eagle cutting across the bright copper arc of the rising sun. It tilted its wings, and soared toward him. He sat motionless. It came near, then banked its wings to swing wide and low around him. It followed the slope to his left and, when it was almost out of sight, suddenly swooped upward, climbing high up the rocky slope.

As it curved back around, he saw what the eagle was hunting. On a ledge high above him, two mountain sheep were grazing. It looked like an ewe and a lamb. The eagle swooped side to side, then quickly dove on the smaller sheep. Before it could move, the eagle had talons hooked into the lamb's back, and was frantically beating its wings to pull the small sheep off balance. In an instant, the sheep had slipped from the ledge, and was airborne. As it fell through the air, it bounced from a jutting rock, then landed with a thud, far down the slope.

The eagle swooped low, and landed on a dead tree trunk, thirty yards above the lamb. There it sat, watching over its kill, making sure it was dead. In a short while, it flew down, and began tearing at the sheep. *Predator and prey... survival of the fittest.*

He glanced back toward town, and saw several people standing in front of the livery. *Almost distracted too long,* he thought, as he reached down for his glass. It was a man, woman, and two girls. And there was a black dog. "That's got to be MacAlan," he whispered.

Soon, the group was walking the trail that cut through the pasture from the livery to Jake's home. He checked his watch... it was ten minutes of seven. Figuring they were going for breakfast, he relaxed, and chewed another piece of the beef, while the eagle continued to tear at the sheep.

He glanced toward Jake's often, not wanting to miss them when they left the house. After a while, he checked his watch again. It was five past eight.

Checking on the eagle, he was amazed at its effort. In an hour, it had torn away the hide from the left side, as the sheep lay on its right, and devoured a good part of the hindquarter, and loin along the backbone. Now, it flew back to the dead tree stump, and sat there considering the remainder of its meal.

Two turkey buzzards had spotted the eagle feasting, and were slowly circling, closer and closer. They were leery to get too close, though, with the eagle still there.

Glancing back to the house, he saw the women come out the door, followed by Jake and MacAlan. When they reached the livery, MacAlan rolled a buggy from under the lean-to roof, while Jake brought a horse from its stall in the livery barn. They harnessed the horse, and MacAlan helped the woman into the buggy.

They waved to Jake, then headed down Main Street, stopping in front of the Post Office. MacAlan went in, and returned with a carton, that he slid in the back of the buggy. Now they were headed west.

Not once, had he had a good opportunity for a shot at MacAlan.

Time to go, he thought. He figured they were headed to the Witten Ranch and, since they traveled more slowly, he could be in his perch south of the ranch before they arrived. He saddled the mustang, packed his gear, and headed west at a gallop. When he reached the overlook, the buggy was already at the ranch. He'd wait and watch.

Eventually, he noticed the dog. It had been laying on the porch, and now rose to its feet. The screen door swung open, and four people came outside. Grabbing his glass, he saw MacAlan, the woman, and the Wittens. Again, MacAlan helped the woman into the buggy, and they headed west. The others were on the porch waving goodbye.

He watched the buggy roll west, then turn north on a seldom traveled trail that would take them into the high country. The trail would eventually lead them up into the area of his shack on the knoll... if they followed it long enough. He knew that country far better than most whites, and certainly better than MacAlan.

They were in his lair now, and he had only to plan where to ambush MacAlan. The woman would merely be a frightened witness to the execution.

Chapter Thirty-Five

Geri and I left the ranch with Will, Julie, and Stumpy waving from the porch. "That's quite a story Stumpy told about his hunt," Geri said.

"It sure was. And I can believe that it made him a life-long friend with the Shoshoni. Depending on the tribe, and their traditions, many Indians feel obligated forever to one who has saved their life "

"Do you think we'll run into any Indians?" she asked, a little nervously.

"Not likely. Not unless they want us to see them for some reason. And there's no need to be concerned for our safety. There hasn't been trouble between the Indians and whites in this area for a few years."

"Good," she said, sounding relieved.

The trail took us through beautiful rock formations and buttes, moving higher into the heavy trees and mountain peaks. Occasionally we crossed large meadows nestled in the thick trees and high peaks. As we rode into one such clearing, Geri nudged me, waving her hand toward some beautiful wildflowers.

"Pretty," I said, then tapped her arm, and pointed in the opposite direction. There, just at the edge of the tree line, stood three bears. It looked like a mother and two growing cubs. For a few moments they stared curiously at us, then the mother turned and loped into the woods, her cubs close behind.

Geri smiled, then whispered, "Wow!"

Farther up the trail, we entered another long, narrow meadow, and saw four elk grazing near the tree line, while seven mule deer stood at the far end studying us warily. I stopped the buggy to watch, but instantly they spooked, and disappeared into the trees.

"I've never seen this much wildlife and beautiful scenery," Geri said.

At one point, the trail squeezed through a thick grove of trees where we had to duck a couple of branches, then around a sharp curve. Suddenly, we were at the edge of a huge, steep drop. Geri gasped, grabbed my arm tightly, and leaned her forehead against my shoulder. I quickly pulled Santa Fe to a stop, and tried to calm Geri.

"It's okay," I said softly. "We're on solid ground, and we won't get any closer to the edge." I patted her shoulder, adding, "When you feel ready, you've gotta see this beautiful view."

She raised her head, looking at me with a nervous grin. Then, squeezing my arm gently, she slowly turned to look. After a brief pause, she whispered, "Oh my!"

Below us, maybe two hundred feet down, was a small, bright blue mountain lake, surrounded by beautiful trees and peaks. We sat in silence, scanning the breathtaking scene. In a short while, she looked back at me again, saying, "I don't know if I've ever seen anything as beautiful."

Looking into her stunning green eyes, I said, "I don't think I have either." Then I realized I was thinking more about her than the landscape.

The trail took us around the steep drop, and to another large plateau' Geri said, "I still can't get over that gorgeous lake back there."

"It's good you got past that sudden fright, too," I told her, with a chuckle.

"Yes. And I'm glad you remained calm." After a few moments, she added, "You remind me of my John. He, too, was a strong man... very calm and gentle."

Waiting for my racing heart to slow down, I finally said, "Thank you. That's very sweet."

"Would you like to see a picture of him?"

"Yes, I would," I replied.

Reaching in her bag, she brought out a beautiful locket. Holding it gently in one hand, she softly stroked it with the other. Then she opened it, and looked at the picture inside, again stroking it lovingly. Holding it up for me to see, she said, "This is my John."

I eased back on the reins. "Whoa, Santa Fe." I gently took the locket from her. Seeing the picture, I said, "He's a very handsome man."

"Yes... he was," she whispered, then smiled softly as she gazed at his picture.

* * *

Scarface sat in the rocks, not eighty yards above and to the side of where the buggy stopped. He'd been there for a half hour.

He knew the trail would lead them to this spot, where he'd have a good long look at them as they approached. He had cut through a ravine, and over a saddle between two peaks, which shaved nearly three miles off the route that the buggy would travel.

He'd been watching them since they'd come around the curve nearly a half mile away. He was letting them get closer and closer, waiting for the right chance to shoot MacAlan. It surprised him when they stopped right in front of him, but he wasn't disappointed. *It's like target practice now*, he thought.

He didn't like that they were directly in front of him, as it only gave a side shot at MacAlan. But he'd take a sitting duck like this anytime. He raised the Sharps rifle, nestled it against his cheek, and lined the sites on Mack's upper chest. *A shot just in front of his arm, would rip through his chest and surely tear up his lungs... or heart... or both.* With the sites steadied on his target, he calmly squeezed the trigger.

* * *

I looked at John's picture for a few more moments, then, moving to hand the locket back to Geri, I fumbled it to the floor of the buggy. Feeling embarrassed, I quickly bent to retrieve it. As my fingers touched the locket, I heard the crack of a rifle shot. The sound I heard next made my heart stop, and I cried out with an agonized, "No-o-o-o!"

The sickening thud of a bullet hitting flesh, was followed by Geri's, "Uhhnn..." as she was slammed sideways in the seat. I spun around, drew my Colt, and fired toward where the shot had come from. I scanned the area, saw nothing, then quickly turned back to check Geri.

196

"Geri... can you hear me?"

She grimaced, and answered with a groan, "Mmmm hmmm."

Her neck was pressed against the side rail of the buggy seat. "Let me ease you up... get your neck off that rail," I said, wrapping her in my arms and slowly lifting.

She moaned, painfully, but when I hesitated, she whispered, "It's okay. Lift me up."

Once I had her upright, I quickly looked for the bullet wound. It had entered just below her shoulder, and came out her back next to her shoulder blade. With my knife, I cut away some of the material from her dress, exposing her shoulder, and her wounds. Then I reached to cut some material from the hem of her dress. As I cut, I lamely tried to joke about it. "Since your dress is already ruined..."

She tried to smile, but it turned to a grimace. Then she whispered, "Not my favorite dress anyway."

I grabbed my canteen, soaked the cloth, then gently sponged the entry wound. There was little bleeding, so I hurriedly moved to the exit wound. I carefully cleaned the area of blood, and some tiny bone chips. Then I rinsed the cloth, and sponged the wound again. As I looked into her questioning eyes, I said, "The only good thing is that it went through cleanly, without much damage. You're going to be okay... hurting... but okay."

Rinsing the cloth out again, I said, "We've got to get you to Doc Undahl. It won't be easy, but we gotta get you there." I folded the cloth, and pressed it against the front of her shoulder. "Can you hold this in place?"

"Yes," she whispered, reaching with her hand.

As I removed my shirt, I explained, "I'm going to fold this, soak it with water, then tuck it into your dress in back. Hopefully it will press against the wound." I slid it in place, and it looked like it would stay.

"As much as you can," I said, "it would help to lean against my shirt to put some pressure on the wound." Then I eased her against the seat.

She nodded. "I'll try." As she said it, she squeezed her eyes closed, showing the pain.

I jumped to the other side of the seat, saying, "Once we get turned around and started back, you can lean your good shoulder against me, and I can help steady you for the trip." With everything she did, or said, I could see the severe pain she was experiencing, how uncomfortable she was, and... how strong and patient she was.

I turned the wagon, and we started for the ranch. She leaned against me, her back pressed against the seat. I wrapped my arm around her. She glanced up at me, and I said, "I'm so sorry."

"For what?" she whispered.

"For getting you into this."

She slowly shook her head. "You couldn't have known."

We were quiet for a long time. Finally, the ranch was in sight, and I saw Patch running toward us. As he neared, I said, "Hey, Patch, how you doin' boy?"

Chapter Thirty-Six

Patch moved along with the buggy, hopping excitedly. "He's so sweet," Geri said softly. Then raising her eyes with pained effort, added, "A little like you."

My heart swelled, and I whispered, "Thank you."

Julie and Will were sitting on the porch, and noticed Patch leave on a run. When we turned through the gate, they sensed something was wrong.

"Geri's been shot!" I shouted.

"Oh no..." Julie exclaimed, getting to her feet, and hurrying down the steps.

Will shouted, "Pull it up here next to the porch," as he waved us over. They helped me get Geri from the buggy, and into their spare bedroom.

"We need to get Doc Undahl," I said. "Is Stumpy out in the barn?" I had noticed his Paint, saddled and standing near the barn door.

"Yeah, I'll get him to hightail it into town," Will said, hurrying out the door.

With Geri sitting on the edge of the bed, Julie said, "Mack, you go sit in the kitchen. Have yourself a shot of whiskey. I'm gonna clean her up."

A little dazed, I finally looked up at Julie, saying, "Oh... yeah... okay."

In the kitchen, I glanced out the door, and saw Stumpy heading down the road at a gallop. Will was headed back to the house, so I stepped out to meet him on the porch. I eased into a chair, saying, "Julie has things under control. All we can do now is wait."

Taking a chair, Will asked, "How did it happen?"

I told him the details, adding, "Had to be Scarface. And I'm sure the bullet was meant for me."

We sat in there in the quiet early evening, thinking on the Scarface problem. In a short while, Julie came to join us. "She's doing well, "she said. "I've got her cleaned up, and in one of my night dresses. I think we should let her rest until Doc gets here."

"Thanks," I said, then retold the whole story for her.

"You're probably right about Scarface," she said. "But... how you gonna find him, or pin anything on him?"

I stared at the porch floor, anger welling in me. "Somehow... some way... he's going to slip up. I'm gonna be there when he does."

In a while, we noticed a dust cloud. "It's probably Stump," Will said, checking his watch. "It's about forty minutes since he left, so I'm guessin' that's him."

Soon we could see that it was Stump, his Paint mare moving at a steady gallop. He turned in the gate and, before the mare came to a full stop at the barn, Stumpy's feet were on the ground, and he was headed toward us. "Doc's right behind," he called out. "I told her what was wrong, and she threw a bunch of stuff in her bag.

"Sit down and catch your breath," Will told him.

"Thanks for being the Pony Express," I said.

He smiled, plopped down on a chair, and blew out a long breath of relief. "I was lucky to catch her before she left on a house call. She was off to see Mrs. Fernley, a few miles east of town. Her baby's due next month, so Doc said that call could wait."

We noticed another dust cloud, and soon could see it was a horse and buggy coming at a trot. "There she is," Stumpy said.

When she turned in the gate, Will was waving her over to the porch. She stopped the buggy, and I reached to help her down. "Thanks, Mack," she said, grabbing her bag, and hurrying up the steps.

Julie held the door open, saying, "Come on in, Ann," then led her to the bedroom where Geri rested.

Will, Stumpy, and I sat on the porch rehashing the story again. Soon Julie joined us, and said, "It looks good. Ann's gonna need to sew her up a bit, but she'll be fine." As she started to sit down, she hesitated, then asked, "Anyone like a cup of coffee with me?"

We all nodded, and Will said, "Let me help."

When they returned, Will held a tray with four cups of coffee, and Julie had a plate of cookies. Soon, Julie was getting up to fetch the coffee pot for refills, when Ann came to the door. "She's doing good," she said. "I had to give her a couple of stitches in the front, and a few in the back to close the wounds, but she's fine."

"I was just getting more coffee," Julie said. "Are you ready for a cup?"

"I sure am," she said, wiping her hands on a towel, and stepping out of Julie's way. "So, Mack..." she continued. "You've probably told the story a few times already, but how about once more for me." She stepped aside again, as Will came out with a chair for her.

"Sure," I said, and, after giving everyone a moment to get settled, began recounting the details... beginning to end.

When I'd finished, Ann asked, "Who is this Scarface? And why is he out to get you?"

"Don't know," I said, shrugging.

Will spoke up. "You've known about all the trouble there's been in the area..."

"Mmm hmm," she responded, nodding, then sipping her coffee.

"Well, Mack has narrowed it down to Scarface as the most likely culprit. So... maybe he caught scent of that, and wants to eliminate Mack as a problem."

She stared at her coffee cup, considering the idea. "That makes some sense, I guess."

"And, unfortunately," I scowled, showing my disgust with it all, "Geri ends up as the innocent bystander... and I feel like I'm to blame."

"I know it's what you feel," Julie said, "but you're not to blame for any of this."

"Oh, so I don't forget," Ann said, looking toward Julie. "Geri's dressings need to be changed every day. I left what you'll need for the next three days, then I'll be back to check on her. That ointment from Mike is good stuff, so use some each time you change the dressing."

Everything seemed to be under control, and Ann was getting ready to leave. I told everyone, "I'm gonna saddle Blaze and ride to Jake's. I need to explain to Jenna and Lauren what's happened, and think I'll suggest they stay there for a few days. I can bring them out to visit her here every afternoon."

Ann agreed. "That's a good idea. Geri's going to need a lot of rest for a couple of days."

As I tightened the cinch on my saddle, I told Blaze and Patch, "You guys need a good workout. You've been relaxing here at the ranch for a few days now. Time for a good run."

Patch tilted his head, as though objecting to the notion that he needed a good run. I swung up in the saddle and, as we headed for the road, I waved to the folks on the porch. Patch had dropped his objection, and was jogging alongside us.

Turning east on the road, I nudged Blaze into a good trot to warm her up. Then just the pressure of me leaning forward in the saddle, saying, "Let's go, girl," was all that was needed to kick her into high gear. In a few strides she was running at full gallop. Patch stretched out, and was running with us, stride for stride. When I thought we were near the halfway point, I eased back, bringing her to a trot, then a walk. I wanted to give them both a breather before running the second half. Patch walked alongside, eagerly glancing up as though to say, *Let's go... I'm ready for more.*

"Good boy, Patch," I said, and his tail began to wag with such energy it almost threw him off his stride.

When we reached Jake's, I leaned over in the saddle to unlatch the gate by the livery. Then, closing it behind me, I steered Blaze toward the house. I tied her to the hitching rail next to their large front porch, and had Patch lay on the porch to wait.

When Sheryl answered the door, she glanced past me, asking, "Where's Geri?"

"There's been an accident. I've come to let you know. Are the girls here?"

"Yes, everyone's here," she said. She stepped aside, and anxiously waved me in the door. "Come in... come in." Then she called out for everyone to join us.

Lauren came around the corner and, when she saw me, gave a cheerful, "Hi, Mack!"

Before I could respond, Jenna said, "Hi. Where's Aunt Geri?"

"Well..." I started, then hesitated. "I've come to let you know there's been an accident."

Before the last word was out of my mouth, Lauren cried, "Oh no!" and had tears already welling.

"She's okay, Lauren," I told her, trying to be as reassuring as I could. "Doctor Undahl has treated her, and says she's doing good."

"What happened?" Jenna asked with apprehension.

I eased into the story, trying not to alarm them. By the time I finished, all four girls were wiping away tears, so I tried again to reassure them. "Your Aunt Geri is a strong lady. She wanted me to tell you not to worry, and that she'll be excited to see you tomorrow afternoon."

Everyone was quiet, so I continued. "Dr. Undahl has given her some good medication so she'll sleep well. For the next few days, it would be better if you stayed here, and I bring you out there to visit each afternoon. She really needs a lot of rest for a couple of days." By now, they were being very understanding, and didn't object to my suggestion.

Cambria said, "Some days we can saddle up and ride out there. You wouldn't have to come in to get us." The girls seemed to like that.

"The good thing is," Sheryl said, "you get to visit us for another week."

Jenna and Lauren were cheering up even more.

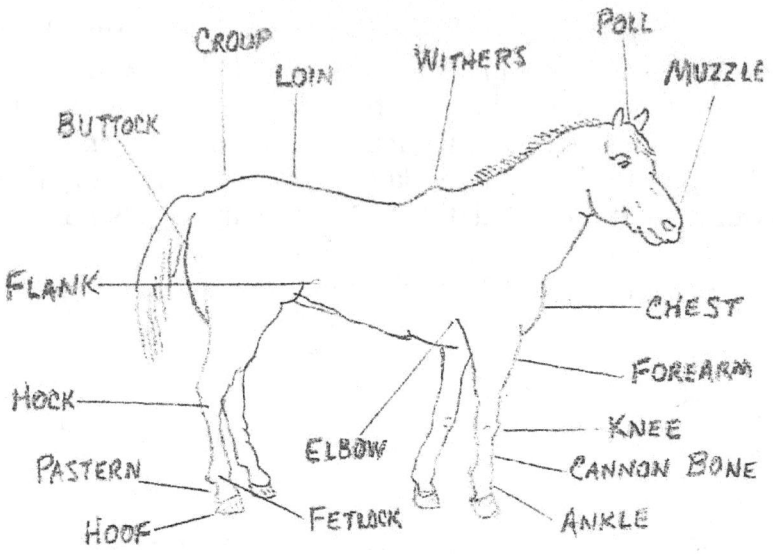

Chapter Thirty-Seven

Next morning at the Witten's, I was up early feeding and saddling Blaze. I was riding out to where the shooting happened to see what I could find. "Maybe I can pick up a trail," I'd said at breakfast.

As I was ready to swing in the saddle, Stumpy asked, "You sure you don't want me to ride along?"

"No, I'll be fine Stump. Don't know if I'll find anything out there anyway... and I'll be careful."

When I reached the spot where I thought I'd stopped the buggy, I swung down and tied Blaze off to the side. "You sit here by Blaze," I told Patch. "So you don't walk over any tracks there might be." He sat, then lay down next to her.

I could see my boot tracks where I'd gone around the buggy to sit on the other side, so Geri could lean against me with her good shoulder. I stood there, gazing up the slope, trying to guess the angle of the shot. About where I figured it should be, there was a cluster of rocks. It was straight out to the side and a little above where the wagon had been sitting. It looked maybe seventy or eighty yards away. *That's gotta be it*, I thought.

Standing among the boulders, I could see it was a good spot to hide. Behind was a slope that dropped down to a stand of pinyon pine, where he could've hidden his mustang. I began to look more closely, trying to see if he'd left any sign. I saw boot tracks up and down the slope. Then, in among the boulders, I caught a glint of light from something shiny.

I knelt to look closer, and saw an empty rifle cartridge. I found a long skinny stick, eased it between the rocks, and slid it into the cartridge. Slowly, I lifted the empty shell from its hiding. *A Sharps .50 caliber*, I thought, then dropped it in my vest pocket.

Finding nothing more around the rocks, I followed the tracks down the slope to the pines. There was an area where he had used a branch from a pinyon to brush away all the tracks where his horse had stood. Two boot tracks and four round impressions were all that remained.

He wrapped his horse's hooves. It's an old trick used by Indians, and others, to avoid leaving a trail. I could make out several of the round impressions where he'd headed out, but quickly lost the trail.

As I started back up the slope, I noticed something different about his tracks that I hadn't seen before. Kneeling and looking closer, I saw a that the toe of his left boot, when it dug into the dirt, left a ragged notch out of the round impression. *A chunk has been torn from the left sole*, I thought, as I traced a track with my fingertip. "Hopefully, your boot betrays you," I whispered.

Sitting there in silence for a while, trying to make sense of something that made no sense, I finally returned to Blaze and Patch. "Let's head back guys." Patch, who was resting off to the side, rose to his feet in one fluid motion and was ready to go.

Geri was healing well, and by the third day she was up and moving around. "I need to get some fresh air and sunshine," she said. Doc Undahl was coming out to see Geri that afternoon, so the Wittens had invited Ann to stay for supper.

In the late afternoon, finished with all the catch-up projects that Stumpy and I had to take care of, I walked over and joined Geri on the porch. I dropped my hat to the floor, and wiped my forehead with my bandana. We relaxed, talking about things — little things, everyday things — then she said, "Take a walk with me."

"Sure." I said, and helped her to her feet.

"Let's stroll back by that grove of trees, and check the apple tree," she said, as she stepped from the porch. We walked and continued our conversation. She was easy to talk with, and easy to be with.

As we walked, she gently took my hand. When we neared the grove of trees, she said, "We'll be leaving for San Francisco soon... probably day after tomorrow, if Ann says I'm okay to travel."

I softly squeezed her hand, saying, "I was afraid that day would come."

We walked in silence for a short while, then she stopped me, turned, and stood close. Looking into my eyes, she raised her arms, wincing as she moved the left one, and took my face in her hands, gently caressing. Searching my face with her eyes, she softly smiled, and said, "I know how you feel about me, and I hope you know how much I care for you."

"Yes, I do know," I said.

"I've had three days to think about us... and I've thought about almost nothing else."

"I..." I began, and she gently held a finger to my lips.

Then she said, "We're from two different worlds, Mack. As much as I love this landscape, I couldn't survive here. Not happily anyway. And you wouldn't be happy in a big city like Chicago." She paused to let me respond... if I wanted to.

I didn't want to. I just stared into her beautiful green eyes, wishing it weren't true. Her soft smile came back again. "I will cherish our having known one another, and be thankful for the days we've shared. I'll never let go of that. You'll always be a part of me."

Her hand slid to my shoulder, and she gently tugged, as her face came toward me. I bent to meet her kiss. Like the touch of her hands, the kiss from her lips was so soft, so gentle, so sensual, it was a moment of thundering tenderness.

I wrapped my arms around her, and gently hugged her. Finally, I whispered, "I know you're right... but I don't want to let go."

She squeezed, and we stood there, quietly holding on. In time, I eased my arms from around her, then took her hand. Walking back, I said, "I know you're right... and you'll always be a part of me, too."

"When we leave San Francisco, and are headed back to Chicago, is it alright if we stop here again? I'd like to see you one more time, say goodbye again, and maybe hear some news about who shot me."

I nodded. "I'd like that, too."

She rose to kiss me on the cheek. "I was hoping you wouldn't say no."

Chapter Thirty-Eight

"This is quite a gathering ," Kristine said, as she patted my shoulder. Seated in her eatery, we were having a going-away-breakfast for Geri and the girls. We met at nine o'clock, and pushed several tables together to seat thirteen of us. The group included Geri and the girls, the Wittens, Stumpy, Jake and his family, Doc Undahl, Mike, and me.

"You leavin' on today's stage?" Kristine asked Geri.

"Yes, at noon. Ann gave me the okay to travel, so we're ready to go see my brother and his family."

"Did she give you something to ease the pain, as you're bumpin' down the trail in that stagecoach?"

Ann pointed to Mike. "Actually, I recommended one of his remedies. It's very good for pain relief."

"Hope to see you again one day," Kristine said, as she turned, and headed for the kitchen.

The morning rolled along with good conversation, and good food. Mike told us of his plan to leave Eagle Bluff. "Probably after the stage pulls out, and I have a chance to say farewell to a few other folks."

"Where are you headed, Mike?" Ann asked.

"Well... there's an old Shoshoni Medicine Man that I haven't seen for five or six years. I'm gonna work my way north and west, see if I can track him down. He's probably up toward the Snake River somewhere.

"He's a very wise and interesting man, and I'd sure like to sit with him again. I learned more about healing from this man, then I did in all my years of medical school education. He has a wealth of knowledge about the use of plants and herbs for many, many things. Knowledge that's been preserved, and handed down through the generations of his people."

After an hour and a half had passed, and we'd finished eating, it was time for goodbyes. Will, Julie, and Stumpy said theirs, and Geri couldn't thank them enough for taking care of her.

Then she grinned at Stumpy, saying, "Remember, if you're ever in Chicago..."

"I'll look you up," he joked, giving her a polite hug.

Jake and his family were next. Again, Geri poured out her thanks for taking such good care of Jenna and Lauren while she healed.

"I hope we'll see you again one day," Sheryl said, giving her a big hug.

"You will!" Lauren said, excitedly. "Aunt Geri said we get to stop here for a day or two on our way back home from San Francisco. And we'll get to visit then for a couple of days."

"That's great!" Sheryl said, just as excited as Lauren now. Then, to Geri, she added, "Be sure to send a telegraph before you leave, so we'll know when to expect you back here."

"I surely will," Geri said, giving her a big hug.

The rest of us left Kristine's, and strolled toward the Overland office to wait for the stagecoach. We relaxed on the benches in front of Paul's office, while the girls walked down Main Street to visit with Kenny Page. Amazingly, they had him involved in an on-going conversation. Something he rarely did.

They had treated him sweetly the whole time they were here and, other than his usual stance of staring down at the street, he was answering their questions, and even giving them a brief smile. It was nice to see him smile.

When he decided that he'd talked long enough, he said, "Bye," and went back to his shoveling.

Paul came out on the boardwalk, and sat down to visit. He said to Geri, "I heard a rumor."

"About what?"

"That you might be stopping by here again in a couple of weeks."

"Yes, we will. Probably for a day or two, before heading on home to Chicago," she said.

"Well, it'll be at least a half-hour before the stage is here, so how about I take a portrait of you and your nieces. I can have prints ready for you when you return."

"Really?" she asked, with some surprise.

"Yup, and it's on me. I'm just getting my studio and processing equipment set up, and trying to take a variety of portraits to get some experience. So, you would be helping me out."

"That's great! Let me call the girls."

We were all eager spectators watching Paul practice his photography. He didn't look like a beginner, as he comfortably went about his business.

I told Jenna, "You need to smile like you really mean it." First she blushed, then her smile was much brighter.

"That's it," I said, grinning at her. "Now you look like you're having fun."

With the portraits taken, we were all back out on the boardwalk waiting for the stage. Paul told us it had stopped there about forty minutes ago to unload passengers and baggage, then went down to Jake's to take on a new team of horses. "It should be back here any minute now."

Soon, we heard the loud voice of the driver, and saw a team of horses swing out from behind the livery. The fresh horses turned up Main Street, and were trotting toward us. Lauren turned to Jake's girls, Cambria and Samantha, and said, "Oh no... I don't want to leave yet."

Everyone shared hugs and goodbyes with Geri and the girls. Feeling sad and empty, I waited until the others were done with their goodbyes. Geri gave a soft smile, and walked over to where I stood.

I told her, "I guess I didn't realize, or want to admit to myself maybe, how hard this would be."

"I know," she said, taking my hand. "It's really hard."

As we talked, the girls stepped over to tell me goodbye. Jenna gave me a big hug, and said, "See you in a couple weeks."

"I look forward to it," I told her.

Then hugging Lauren, I said, "You be sure to have lots of fun in San Francisco."

"We will," she said, and turned to board the stage.

Looking up into my eyes again, Geri said, "Well, I guess it's time." Then she rose to her tip-toes, and kissed my cheek.

I hugged her and, trying to brighten the mood, said, "See you in a couple weeks."

She slowly looked down, and told me, "I've gotta climb on board before I start crying."

With everyone aboard, the driver, Smiley, climbed into the box, and grabbed two fists full of reins. "Let's go Billy," he shouted to one of the lead horses. "Gitt-up thar." He tapped them with the reins, and steered them away from the boardwalk. Their heads bobbed and their hooves kicked up dust, as they leaned into the harnesses. Finally, the stagecoach creaked and began to roll.

Arms were waving out the coach windows, and I could hear shouts of goodbye. Waving back, and returning the goodbyes, I noticed one hand waving slowly, almost sadly, and felt the painful emptiness again.

I decided I'd take a long, slow, round-about ride back to the ranch. Time to think about things. Time to begin healing the empty feeling inside. When I was finally in sight of the ranch, Patch came running to greet me. As usual, he hopped, and wagged his whole body with excitement. He lifted my spirits.

"You're such a character, Patch," I said. "It's nice being missed so much."

That afternoon, Mike stopped on his way out of town. We visited on the porch, and Stumpy asked him, "What's that Medicine Man's name? The one you're wanting to try to find up north."

"DosaWeda is his name. 'Grizzly Bear' is about as close as I get in translation."

"Well, tell ol' Grizz to say hello to Cameahwait for me.

"I hope I'm able to, Stump." He checked his watch and added, "It's about time I head out."

"When will you be back this way again?" Julie asked.

"Next summer, I hope."

"You be sure to stop and say hello," she insisted.

"I'll plan on it," he said, nodding.

As he climbed into his wagon seat, I shook his hand, saying, "See you next year, Mike."

"Until that time, Mack. Until that time."

Chapter Thirty-Nine

A few hours had passed since Mike left. We had eaten supper, and were sitting on the porch again, talking about the ranch work we needed to catch up on. I held up a finger, interrupting our conversation. "Hear that?" I said. "It's horse's hooves coming fast."

"You're right," Will answered, as he leaned forward in his chair, listening intently.

We moved to the porch rail, but saw nothing in the dimming, late evening light. Finally, I could see Sarah Jane pulling Mike's wagon, and comin' like the devil was hot on their trail.

They wheeled through the gate, barely slowing, then pulled to a sliding stop. Dust was flyin' and, before the wheels had come to rest, Mike leaped from the wagon, and was running toward us.

I called out, "What is it?"

Panting, he shouted, "It's Scarface! I saw his white Mustang."

"Come over and catch your breath," Will said.

"Grab a chair," Julie told him.

He sat, and blew out his breath a couple of times, trying to calm himself. Finally, he explained, "I was gonna take the trail north... the one that's a mile and a half the other side of the Kennedy place." He paused, and gulped another deep breath.

"As me and Sarah Jane rolled past their place, I saw several horses hitched to the rail by their front porch. Pat's dapple gray was there, and I figured they all must be gathered there for supper.

"Then, as we moved on down the trail, I glanced back through some pinyon pines behind their barn, and caught a glimpse of a white horse. First thing that come to mind was Scarface."

"Did you see him?" I asked, anxiously.

"No, I didn't. I eased Sarah Jane to a stop, then climbed down, and walked to where I had a better look. It was a white mustang all right, with a black saddle. The mustang knickered with a low, growling sort of whinny. But I don't think anyone inside the home heard it. I could still see most of the porch, and nobody came outside for a look-see."

"Something about that doesn't seem right," I said.

"Didn't to me either," he agreed.

Rising from my chair, I told them, "Think I'll git on over there. See if he's still around." Not saying more, not even goodbye, I leaped off the porch, and hurried to saddle Blaze. I pulled the cinch tight, dropped the stirrup and stuck my boot in it.

"Be careful," Julie pleaded.

"I will," I assured her, then grabbed the reins, swung my leg over, and spurred Blaze into a gallop. Patch soon took the lead, and we were at full stride, kickin' up a dust trail and moving fast.

As we neared the Kennedy place, I eased Blaze to a trot. Across the trail from their house is a stand of pinyon, juniper, and a few cottonwoods. We veered through the trees, hoping not to be seen or heard.

When we were beyond the barn, I spotted a patch of white through a gap in the trees, just like Mike had said. I slid from the saddle and, grabbing my rifle, told Patch, "You stay here and protect Blaze."

He gave a soft whine from deep in his throat, as though to tell me, *I'm goin' with you.*

I reached down to scratch him behind his ears, saying, "Someone's got to guard her. Protect her from mountain lions and such. So, you stay here, and keep alert."

He glanced up at Blaze, back at me, then slowly laid near the tree where she was tied. I quietly worked my way toward the mustang. A couple of times he knickered an alarm, but I saw no one. I moved slowly, pausing often, scanning the area. When I reached the mustang, I patted him on the neck, and scratched his cheeks. After that, he was calm and quiet.

I worked my way to the corner of the barn to get a view of the house. I saw the horses at the hitching rail, and it did look like the whole family had gathered there for supper. I couldn't see movement anywhere, but decided against going closer. *Going this way was out in the open too much, and for too long*, I thought. *Too much risk of being spotted.*

I moved quietly to the other end of the barn. This side of the house held the bedrooms, and there were fewer windows to be spotted from. *Time to see what's going on in there.*

I took a deep breath, let it out slowly, then scooted to the house. The first window showed a dark bedroom, with only a faint light coming through the open doorway. I moved to the next window, and saw the same. The back side of the house had one more window, and I could see that room was dark as well.

Looking around the far side, there were three windows casting light to the ground. The first was next to a back door that led to the pantry and storeroom. From there, you turn right to the kitchen, or left to the dining room. I carefully tried the door, and found it unlocked, but decided not to go in yet.

Moving to the next window, and taking off my hat, I leaned to peek through a gap in the curtains. I flinched, and jerked back. Scarface was right there at the window. He hadn't seen me though.

I paused, trying to settle my nerves, then leaned to look through the curtains a second time. I could see him pacing back and forth, talking to the others. Then it registered, *No, he's not talking with them, he's shouting at them.*

. . .

Earlier that evening, the Kennedys were sitting down for supper. It was to be a memorial of sorts, for Conner on the first anniversary of his death. They would finally try to set aside the ill feelings, and bad memories, and let his soul rest in peace.

At least that's what they thought was the reason for their gathering. After all, each of the boys had received a note inviting them to dinner, telling them the reason for the gathering. And... Kate and Brendan had received a note from Patrick explaining the same.

So it became very confusing when Kate told Patrick, "Your note said..."

"My note?" Patrick interrupted. "We each received a note from you, inviting us, and explaining the reason for getting together."

Just then, Scarface stepped in from the back porch, where he'd stood listening to their confusion. "Hello everyone," he said. "Please sit down."

Startled, confused, and looking up the barrel of a sawed-off shotgun, they all took a seat. Kate slowly sat in her chair, stared at their intruder, and gasped. Then, in astonishment, she exclaimed, "Conner?"

"Yes, mother. How did you know?"

"I'd know those eyes anywhere," she insisted. "How... what..." She stumbled, dumbfounded.

He held up his hand, saying, "Shush, mother, I'll do the talking."

Ignoring that statement, Brendan asked, "How are you still alive?"

"Good question, Father," Scarface said. "An obvious question, but a good one nonetheless. Before I explain, we've got some things to take care of."

"Mother, you get to tie your sons and husband to their chairs." Walking over and handing her some pieces of rope, which she reluctantly took, he continued. "Tie their ankles together, and throw the rope under the chair. Then pull it tight, and tie their wrists tight behind them.

"And let me warn you, dear mother..." he said, glaring at her. "You'll do a good job of tying them. If I check, and find any not tied good and snug, I'll start chopping off fingers. Then they'll have no desire to try untying ropes, now will they?" He showed an evil smile.

"As for the rest of you dear boys... try anything, anything at all, and your mother is the first to go. Then I'll take down whoever I can. So, let's be behavin' ourselves."

As Kate tied the first of her sons, Conner moved to the front door, and took down the four holsters hanging on pegs. It was the custom at the Kennedy House, that when you entered, you removed your hat and gun belt, and hung them on a peg. Never taking his eyes from his family, he threw the guns out the back door.

Kate had tied Adam and Sean, and was now starting with Patrick. Checking the first two, Conner found them snugged up tight. "Good job, Mother. I guess you didn't want them to lose any fingers."

Finished with tying the men in her family, Kate sat back in her chair. Conner, warily watching all of them, laid the shotgun down on the floor, and began tying her ankles. Finished, he checked the ropes on all of them once more. Content that they were secure, he laid the shotgun on the table, pulled up a chair, and relaxed.

Chapter Forty

"How is it that I'm alive, yer wonderin'...."

Conner was staring at his shotgun, not speaking to any one of them in particular. "I suppose it was a stroke of fate." He rose from his chair, and began pacing, slowly circling his captive audience.

"Let's start back before my ugly incarceration." He turned, circling in the other direction. "You see, Father, I knew all about your discovery, and your plans, right from the start. I knew you'd found gold along Rush Creek. I'd quietly follow you there, and you never suspected. I even mined a little of the gold, and had it assayed for myself. Good grade ore it was, too.

"Then I learned about your insistence that everyone in the family keep me in the dark about the whole thing. 'Don't let Conner ruin the plan, like he's ruined so many other things.'" He was pacing faster now, with heavy footsteps.

"A good plan you had, buying up the ranches along Rush Creek before you start mining. That way, no one could be crowdin' in on your gold. You'd have the run of things up and down the creek.

"That gave me the first inspiration for a plan to get revenge on this whole family... to ruin your reputation, and make you as hated as I was. I was the one behind all of the trouble the ranchers had while you tried to buy them out. And it worked. It helped force them into selling to you, adding to the wealth my family, and made the locals despise and hate you.

"Meanwhile, don't 'cha know, I'm workin' on my own clever plan to take control of everything. But, damned if I didn't get myself tossed in prison before I could hatch my plan. And then, to rub salt in the wound, you didn't have a decent word to say about me at the trial, nor ever once enter the prison to pay a visit." He was getting even more agitated, pacing faster, waving his hands, and poking his finger in the air.

"One night, sitting there in that little outhouse of a prison cell, I had a flash of brilliance. There were two problems to solve. First one was how to get out of prison. The second... how to take over the Kennedy properties, and all the gold. The solution was so obvious that I didn't see it right there in front of me." He was calming now, pacing much slower.

"The solution... bribe the Warden. He could free me, and help me eliminate all of you, making me the sole heir to the Kennedy estate. After several meetings with Warden Fitzig, I had him convinced of the value of the land and gold I would inherit, and he'd be a forty percent partner. He began to imagine wealth beyond anything he'd ever dreamed. He was not only a willing accomplice, he was chomping at the bit. He could taste it.

"It was the perfect plan. That is until Ed LaRock took a serious disliking to me. When he cornered me with a homemade knife, he cut me bad, then caught me with a punch that knocked me out. I found out the rest when I woke up in the infirmary the next day. When I was out on the floor, he grabbed a kerosene lamp, poured the kerosene on my face, then threw his lighted cigarette butt at me. Luckily, there was a bucket of water nearby, and one of the guys doused the flames. Otherwise, I was a goner." He paused, passing a hand over his scarred face.

"So, once again, life put a crimp in my plans. But when he saw I would survive, the Warden, fortunately, came up with a great idea to make it all work. He had me pronounced dead, then secretly moved me to the Carson City Hospital.

"The story would eventually be told that this was done to protect me from LaRock, and from his brothers in Virginia City. There is a full pardon in my file, so when I step forward to claim my inheritance I'll be a free man, with Warden Fitzig as witness to who I really am. Michael O'Conner has been my cover name.

"So now step two... the tragic death of my family, leaving me sole heir to their considerable estate. The plan began with the notes to each of you."

. . .

I listened outside the window, straining to hear what Scarface was ranting about. I had to create a diversion to get him away from the Kennedys. To go in while he was holding the shotgun would be foolhardy. No telling how many he'd cut down before I got him... or he got me.

I needed a way to get him out on the porch. Buy a few seconds time. With my mind churning, I noticed a dead tree limb on the ground. It was five feet long, and big around as my arm. *Get that to drop on the porch, maybe it'd do the job,* I thought. I remembered seeing a coil of rope on a peg in the back porch. I moved to the door, slowly slipped it open, then lifted the rope from the peg.

On my way to the front porch, I grabbed the limb, and tied one end of the rope to it. I balanced it against the house so that, when I twitched the rope, it would slide down the house and slap the deck. Then I'd quickly pull it from the deck, and out into the darkness, so Scarface wouldn't immediately see what had caused the noise.

With everything rigged, I quietly eased onto the back porch. Ready to twitch the rope, I mentally crossed my fingers and prayed for help. When I tugged the rope, the limb did its job. It slapped the deck loudly, then I yanked it into the darkness and stepped in the door.

Inside I heard, "What the..." followed by hurried footsteps toward the front door. When I heard the door click open, I peeked to check what was happening. Scarface was holding the door open, warily scanning the area. When he turned to check on his captives, I quickly ducked back.

Hearing what I thought was a footstep on the porch, I chanced another look around the door post. He was slowly stepping out, shotgun held in both hands. As he moved from the door, I hurried through the dining room, quietly as I could. Passing the table, I held a finger to my lips, and noticed Brendan nod his head.

At the door, I listened a moment, then looked to see where he'd gone. He was off the porch, and looking around the corner, shotgun still at the ready. He glanced back, saw me, and swung the shotgun. I jerked back just as the shot ripped away chunks of the door frame, and splintered the door. That was followed by a blast through the large front window, shattering and spraying glass everywhere. The next thing I heard was a shot from his Colt revolver that shattered more glass. I waited, listening. *Maybe he's out of shotgun shells.*

226

Quick as I could, I glanced out the door. There was no sign of him. He must have backed into the darkness. When I looked a second time, a shot rang out. But I was already pulling back, and the bullet ripped through the door and wall.

I reached around the door frame, blindly firing a shot in his direction. I paused, then reached out to fire once more. He must've been watching for the second one, and fired at me just as my shot went off. His bullet tore through my shirt sleeve, burning the skin on my upper arm. I jerked back, like pulling away from a hot branding iron, then checked the damage. It burned like the dickens, but there wasn't much blood.

With everything quiet for a few moments, I pulled my knife, then ducked down, and scooted quickly to Brendan. I placed it in his hand, whispering, "Stay low."

I hurried back to my spot between the door and window. As I rose up, I could see Brendan was working the knife, cutting through the ropes. Soon his hands were free, and he began cutting the rope from his ankles. He crawled over to Patrick, began cutting his ropes, and whispered, "Get to the living room, and start loading. Stay low."

In their living room is a gun cabinet, a fine piece of furniture made of cherry wood. It held four rifles, and three shotguns. The wide drawer across the bottom held boxes of ammunition for each weapon.

Brendan freed the rest and, as they crawled toward the living room, I continued to look for Scarface. I took my hat from my head, placed it over my Colt, then eased it out the door. My hand quivered as I waited for a shot.

Nothing.

Putting the hat back on my head, I reached out into the dark with my Colt. Then, anxiously glancing around the door frame, I hoped my head wasn't the target he was waiting for.

Again, nothing.

"Where are you?" I whispered to the empty darkness. I quickly moved back inside, and turned the kerosene lamp to a faint glow. Then, as I moved past the door to the living room, I said in a louder whisper, "Turn the lamp down low, and wait there."

Moving quietly as I could, I stepped toward the back porch and kitchen. My nerves on edge, and my colt ready to fire, I checked the porch door. It was still closed, and I reached to slide the bolt so that he couldn't come in without plenty of noise to warn us. I quickly turned down the kitchen lamp, and backed away into the shadows, listening hard for any sound from outside.

Still nothing.

I joined the Kennedys, who were huddled behind a large sofa, out of view from the window and door. Surprisingly, none seemed frightened. Kate whispered, "I wish there was a way to save my son, but I think that's hopeless. We have to save the rest of us. How can we do it, Mack?"

"We need to..." I started to say, then froze. I saw a flicker of light reflect off the window, then caught the faint smell of kerosene and smoke. I held up my hand as I looked all around. "Wait here," I said.

When I reached the kitchen, the window was filled with flames. The outside walls were ablaze, and the air held the smell of kerosene. I hurried to the living room, and asked Brendan to check the bedrooms. Then I knelt down to think for a moment.

Brendan returned, saying, "They're on fire, too."

Sean whispered, "Out the front door."

I caught his arm. "Wait Sean. He's got the whole back of the house in flames, so he's got to be out front, waiting to pick us off as we come out the door."

"What do we do?" Kate asked, matter-of-factly.

"We have to get out alright, before the smoke gets us. And I think our best chance is on a dead run. I'm going to distract him. I'll go out the back door and, when you hear me shoot, you charge out the front door.

"Adam, you and Sean lead the way with those shotguns. As you cross the deck, fire a shot into the trees. If he takes my bait, you'll have some idea where he is. And, whether you know where he is or not, fill the air with lead. Make him flinch.

"Go out runnin', and don't stop 'til you reach that thick grove near the road."

Chapter Forty-One

As I rushed toward the back porch, I could feel the increasing heat. I grabbed a broom and knocked the bolt latch open. Then I grabbed a rag, bunched it, and took firm hold of the hot door handle. Shielding my eyes, I swung the door open, and a whoosh of hot air and flames filled the doorway.

I back-stepped, pulled my hat from my head, and took a deep breath. With the Stetson covering my face, I lunged through the flames. I knew I'd be landing blindly, and would likely stumble. I cleared the flames, felt a rush of cool evening air, then pulled my hat aside, all in the blink of an eye. When my boot caught the edge of the step, I stumbled, hit the ground, and rolled. I caught myself, pushed up on one knee, then drew my gun and fired two quick shots. Hopefully, wherever he was, the shots would startle Scarface, and draw his attention.

It worked.

I saw a muzzle blast, then heard the explosion of his pistol. The bullet ripped a chunk of bark from a tree just over my shoulder. In the next instant, I heard a shotgun blast, quickly followed by another. The Kennedys were on their way out the front door.

I drew back the hammer of my Colt, ready to fire at him again. Then I flinched and ducked, when out of the black sky, a lightning bolt split a nearby tree. That was followed immediately by an ear-busting, bone-rattling clap of thunder. In moments, the sky opened up, and dumped a deluge on us.

Scarface had been distracted, too, but now began firing toward his fleeing family. In the darkness, I saw fire leap from the end of his gun barrel, and took aim where I thought he'd be standing. When I squeezed off the shot, I heard a muffled, "Uhhnn."

He's hit, I thought.

That thought hadn't fully cleared my mind, when I saw another muzzle blast, then heard the gunshot. Something slammed me hard in the chest near my left shoulder. I felt a burning pain tear through me. Soon a warm, damp wetness began soaking the back of my shirt. I knew it wasn't the rain doing that.

Realizing I'd been hit hard, and was feeling a little disoriented, I struggled to regain my balance, and clear my head. In the midst of all this, my brain said, *He's fired six shots... He's empty!*

In the brightness of another lightning flash, I saw that he was wounded. Wounded, yes, but raising his gun, aiming again. *Was he out of bullets, or not.*

I quickly aimed my gun, but too late. I heard a shot, and braced for another slam to my body. I knew it would be another painful, burning thud.

When the blow didn't come, I felt relief, and quickly moved so I wasn't the same sitting target. In the next flash of lightning, I glanced around, but didn't see him. *He's moved, too.*

Before my brain finished processing that thought, it told me what I'd really seen, but hadn't quite registered. *He's not gone... he's on the ground.*

232

Out in the darkness, unknown to me, Brendan had been moving through the trees, closer and closer. He felt the responsibility to stop Conner, and clung to the hope he wouldn't have to shoot him. He'd seen Conner's shot that hit me and, when he saw Conner ready to shoot me a second time, he squeezed the trigger of his Winchester.

The bullet hit Conner just behind his left arm, ripped through him, and exploded out his chest. It slammed him to the ground, where he breathed his last. In agony, Brendan dropped to his knees, his eyes squeezed shut.

I stumbled to where Conner lay, and pulled the gun from his hand, making sure there'd be no more shooting. Then I saw Brendan, his hands covering his face, and his shoulders heaving with sobs. In moments, Kate reached him and knelt to hold him.

I looked down at Conner's revolver, wondering, *Was he out of bullets*? I pulled the hammer to half-cock, and flipped open the loading gate. One by one, I shook the empty cartridges from the cylinder. Finally, the sixth one, a heavy bullet, fell into my hand. I felt a shiver run through me, as I stared at what could have been the fatal shot. Discarding the five empties, I squeezed the loaded bullet tightly in my palm, then pressed my fist to my forehead. I said a prayer of thanks that I'd been spared, and knew how indebted I was to Brendan for the pain he'd taken on himself to save my life. When I reach them, I quietly placed a hand on his shoulder. He slowly looked up at me, and I couldn't think of a single word to say in response to the pleading look in his eyes.

I reached under his arm, helping Kate raise him to his feet. When I flinched, Kate said, "You're the one that's in need of help."

Thankfully, the downpour had doused the flames, and we moved back inside. As Kate fetched supplies for treating my wounds, I realized I was still clutching the bullet. I eased my grip, opened my hand, and stared at it once again. A glass of water sat on the table, so I tilted my hand, and watched it role from my palm, then splash into the water. I heard a muffled clink as it hit the bottom of the glass.

Kate returned, and began working on my wounds. "Thankfully, the bullet missed your lung," she said. "It might have chipped a piece of your shoulder blade on the way out, but that's not life-threatening. Your lung would have been."

She folded two clean pieces of cloth, and had me hold one on the front wound, while Brendan held the other over the back wound. Then she took long strips she'd torn from sheet, and began wrapping them snugly around me.

"You're wrapping that poor boy six-ways-till-Sunday, Kate!" Brendan told her, smiling.

"Oh you..." she said with a smirk. "You mind your manners. He needs to be snugged up tight." It was the first light moment since this tragedy started.

As she finished wrapping, I looked at Brendan. His deep pain still showed in his eyes. After a long moment, I told him, "Thanks... for saving me the way you did. I can only imagine how hard that choice was for you."

He considered it, then said, "I could have lost my whole family if not for you. It was a choice I had to make."

Chapter Forty-Two

Over the coming days, I was resting and recuperating in my bed. Patch lay on the floor beside me the whole time. Stumpy made me re-tell the story every evening, while he smoked a cigarette, and sipped a double shot of whiskey. Each time through the story, he seemed just as amazed by the events, and just as surprised by the ending.

Stoney had ridden over to Carson City to arrest Warden Fitzig. The Warden didn't resist, and Stoney had him held in their city jail. He'd later be moved to Eagle Bluff to stand trial for murder, and conspiracy to commit murder.

At trial, Fitzig confessed to everything, and pleaded for the mercy of the court that he not be sentenced to the Nevada State Prison, where he'd served as warden for more than thirty years. The court complied. He was given a life sentence, to be served at the newly opened Folsom State Prison in Folsom, California.

The Warden also told of the place where Conner lived. "I think Mick, 'er Conner that is, killed ol' Sniffy, then took over the place."

By now I was feeling pretty good, ready to get out and about. I asked Stoney if he'd like to ride over, and check out Sniffy's place. The next morning, he was at the ranch to have breakfast before we headed out.

The place was pretty much as the Warden had described, and we found the box of personal items, along with the cash. Among the personal items, was a letter from Sniffy's nephew, who lived near Minneapolis, Minnesota.

Stoney sent him a letter explaining everything about Sniffy's belongings. The nephew telegraphed back, saying he'd arrive in six days. He hoped the Sheriff could show him the property.

When he arrived, Stoney borrowed a buggy from Jake, and took the nephew, a Mr. Arthur Bjorn, out to Sniffy's. As they stood near the shack, scanning the area, Art said, "He had quite a little place on this knoll."

Knowing he'd not likely keep the property, Art had brought along a large piece of wood, and some paint. He made a sign that read:

3000 Acres For Sale
Contact Sheriff Dawson, Eagle Bluff

He showed Stoney, saying, "With your permission."

"That's alright by me," Stoney answered, and helped him nail it to a nearby tree, where it would be easily seen by any passer-by.

"If anybody's interested, you know how to reach me. And I plan on paying you a fee, just like a Land Office would get."

"That won't be necessary," Stoney told him, shaking his head.

"I insist. Otherwise, I'd have to be paying someone I don't trust as much as I do you."

Eventually, a couple from the area north of Sniffy's, who were friends of the Shoshoni and the Paiutes, bought the place. They loved the solitude.

Feeling healthy, and going strong again, I was helping Stumpy with some of the ranch work. One evening Brendan and Kate stopped by to introduce themselves to Will and Julie. As they visited over coffee, the Kennedys invited all of us to a Saturday afternoon get-together they were having.

"We're cookin' a hog over open fire," Kate said. "And there'll be plenty of other food to go with it."

"There'll even be some good music," Brendan added.

"It'd be our pleasure," Will told them. "We'll be there by mid-afternoon."

Their party was a grand success. They'd invited Jake and his family, Stoney and his, Jeff from the gun shop, Myron the barber, and all four of us from the Witten Ranch. The Kennedys were trying to heal the old wounds, and make a fresh start with the local folks. And it worked.

The following Saturday, Brendan stopped to see Will. "Got a few minutes?" he asked.

"Sure do. Have a seat." Will pointed to a porch chair, asking, "How 'bout a cup of coffee?"

"That'd be fine," Brendan said, taking a seat.

In a short while, Julie brought coffee and cookies. Giving her a smile, Brendan said, "Thanks so much."

After a time of visiting, Will asked, "Was there something particular you wanted to talk about, Brendan?"

"Yes, there is," he answered. "I wanted to talk about your land."

Will felt his heart sink with great disappointment, thinking, *Trying to buy us out, again*? Finally, he asked, "What about it?"

"You've got a mighty fine spread here."

"Yeah, we think so too."

"And, you do a right good job of ranchin' it."

"Thank you..." Will said, slowly, wondering where this was headed.

"Well, Kate and I figure you and Julie are just about the best neighbors a body could ask for. So we hope you stay put, and continue to be our good friends."

Will felt his whole body lift with relief, and a smile creased his face. "We plan to do that very thing," he said, reaching to shake Brendan's hand.

Then, as though remembering something, Brendan added, "Oh... you know about the gold I found, just four miles up the creek from your land."

"I heard about that."

"Well, there's good reason to think that there could be gold down-stream, maybe on your place here. If you've a mind to, I know a little of the geology, and what to look for, and I'd be glad to help you with some prospectin' to see if you might have a bit of your own ore."

Will leaned back in his chair, pleasantly surprised, then said, "That's mighty fine of you, Brendan. We'd like that a lot."

Brendan did help them find gold, and then warned them, "This will bring you a small fortune. Get yourself ready. It can throw you way off balance."

They heeded his advice, and began making plans for their future. Plans that included building a new school house near Eagle Bluff, where Julie would help teach.

Making Aldus Ambrose Giles a one-third partner was also in the plan. Stumpy reacted by saying, "You don't have to do that."

Julie told him, "We know... but that's what we're going to do."

"Not sure I'll know how to behave as a rich fella," he joked.

240

Chapter Forty-Three

Life in Eagle Bluff seemed considerably brighter these days, and past tensions had disappeared. The Kennedys were generous neighbors, ready to help anyone in need.

New-found wealth hadn't changed the Wittens — not the kind of people they were, nor the way they lived their lives. But it did give them the ability to help others, and help Eagle Bluff grow with projects like the school.

Their generosity in making Stumpy a partner, had allowed him to help his sister and her family. They were near losing their farm in Nebraska. Stump paid up all their back payments, and bought them a new team of plow horses, the biggest need they had on their farm. It was amazing to see how it made Stumpy feel — being able to help them that way.

Meanwhile, I was completely healed, and back to full strength. Life was good.

Finished with the ranch chores, I saddled Blaze and, with Patch at our side, headed to town on some errands. The bright orange, morning sun was beautiful, and I tugged my Stetson low on my forehead to shade my eyes. The hills and mountains wore a blanket of sunlight that was creased by deep, shadow-filled ravines.

When I reached Eagle Bluff it was near noon, so I headed to Kristine's in hopes there was someone I could join for dinner. As I stepped in, the wonderful smells of baked ham, fresh bread, and coffee lit my appetite. I heard Jake's big voice calling, "Hey, Mack, come on over."

Pulling out a chair for me, Stoney said, "You're just in time. We were about to order."

When I sat down, our waitress, Karlee, walked over. "Hi, Mack, would you like coffee?"

"Sure thing, Karlee."

As we ate, we visited about all the latest happenings. I'd ordered the baked ham that I'd smelled when I walked in the door, along with mashed potatoes smothered in a thick, rich gravy Kristine had made from the ham's juice.

Stoney told us of an outbreak in cattle rustling. It seemed to be spread through Nevada, Montana, and Wyoming. "Rustlers are hitting ranches at night, cutting out forty or fifty head of cattle, making it easy to move them through the darkness. Sounds like there's been a dozen ranches hit so far. Luckily, none close by here."

He paused to sip his coffee, then continued. "The government is notifying every Sheriff and U.S. Marshall west of the Mississippi. So let your friends and neighbors know to be on the lookout."

Jake said, "Oh... hey...." Then, looking at Stoney, he apologized. "Sorry to interrupt, and change the subject on you, but we got a telegram this morning."

Looking at me, he said, "Geri and the girls will be stopping here next week.

"Really!" I said, sounding excited, which I was. But it also hid the feelings I'd been wrestling with the past couple of days.

"Yeah. They'll be here Tuesday on the morning stage. They plan to stay two nights at the hotel, then leave on the afternoon stage Thursday."

"Thanks Jake. I'll have to plan on being here." I said it, smiling, though I wasn't sure just what I'd be doing.

That night, I lay on my bed, staring into the silent darkness. The darkness was softened by moonlight slipping through the gap in the window's curtain. The silence was ruffled by Stumpy's snoring. Thankfully, he wasn't one of those loud, keep-you-up-all-night, kind of a snorers.

I'm a very sound sleeper, and usually out in minutes. But this was the third night in a row I lay staring for many hours, before finding sleep. I was having troubling dreams that I couldn't remember after waking. Dreams that left me with an uneasy feeling of needing to leave.

Adding to all this turmoil, were my unsettled feelings for Geri. She held a special place in my heart and, though wishing things could have worked out differently, I had resolved to live with those feelings as treasured memories. I wasn't sure that seeing her again would add to or take away from the memories, but I knew I didn't want to face saying goodbye to her again, this time forever.

Then there was my situation here. When I first came, there seemed to be an undercurrent of tension, which was a challenge to unravel. Now, even though the Wittens and Stumpy are like family, I knew I wouldn't be content continuing on as a ranch hand, no matter how well paid.

So, everything seemed to be telling me it was time to try a place that's new. Finally, feeling like it was what I had to do, I let my mind settle, and slipped into that marvelous unknown we call sleep.

243

Stumpy woke me in the early morning with a loud cough. I opened my eyes, and saw him propped on the side of his bunk, rolling a cigarette — his usual routine to start the morning. I yawned and stretched, pushed myself up at the side of my bed and put my feet on the floor. I rubbed my eyes, saying, "You gotta quit those things one day, Stump. Before that cough gets worse."

"Yeah... I probably should," he replied, staring at the cigarette he was about to light.

Patch eased up to me, put his head on my knee, and gave me a look of, *How 'bout some attention here.*

"You're such a good guy, Patch," I told him. I stroked his head, scratched around his ears and neck.

Dressed and grabbing my hat — a man can't start the day without his hat — I heard Will shout from the porch, "Come 'n get it." That meant breakfast was hot.

When we walked in the door, I immediately saw that Julie was cookin' my favorite breakfast. Whenever she had leftover ham, she'd chop it into small chunks. Then she'd chop up some onions, green peppers, and cheese. Scrambling three eggs, she poured them into a hot frying pan. As they began to cook, she sprinkled the chopped goodies over the top. Just before the eggs were fully cooked, she folded it in half to hold all the goodies inside. That, along with a slice of toast off the griddle, and a hot cup of coffee... man-oh-man, there's no better breakfast.

As we ate, my mind was churning, searching for the right words. I was trying to find the right way to tell them I'd decided it was time to move on. Finally, I just blurted out, "I'm gonna be leavin' this mornin'."

244

Will stopped chewing to ask, "Where are you off to?" He asked it as though I was running to town, or on some errand.

"No..." I started to say. Then, after a long pause, I finished the thought. "I mean that I'm leaving here... moving on."

Stumpy choked, then shouted, "You can't be."

Julie put down her fork, covered her mouth for a moment, then asked, "Why, Mack?"

"Well... it's nothing that anyone's done," I said. "Certainly nothing you guys have done. Being shot makes you think about your mortality, and I know there's things I still want to do, places I still want to see."

They were all silent for a few moments, then Will spoke up. "You gotta do what your heart tells ya. We're sure gonna miss you around here though."

"I'm gonna miss you guys an awful lot, too." I was trying not to get emotional, but was already feeling it.

"What about Geri?" Julie asked, sadly.

I stared into my coffee cup, thinking about the question, then finally explained. "Actually, that's part of the reason I'm leaving now. I've struggled with the whole notion of seeing her again, only to have to say goodbye again... this time forever."

She nodded, smiling sadly. It gave me a sense that she understood. "What do you want us to tell her when we see her?"

"Two things, I guess. First, that she knows how I feel about her, but that I'm a coward and don't want to say goodbye again... forever. Second, that I'm off to track down an uncle and cousin, probably the only family I have left. I think she'll understand."

That second part wasn't the truth, but it was a lot easier than trying to explain all my confusion and mixed feelings about moving on. And, about where I'd be headed. I still wasn't sure about any of it myself.

Chapter Forty-Four

As I saddled Blaze, Julie came to give me a big hug. "Thank you, for all that you've done. It will feel a little empty around here without you, Mister MacAlan."

"Thanks. I'll miss you, too, Julie."

Will shook my hand, then did something a stoic cowboy seldom does. He wrapped his other arm around me, and gave me a hug. "You know you're always welcome here, friend."

"Thanks, Will. I'll always be proud to call you friend."

Finally, Stumpy reached to shake my hand, slapping me on the shoulder with his other hand. "I guess it's back to being lonely in that bunkhouse again," he joked.

"I suppose," I said, grinning. "But only 'till you get that little house built on the rise over yonder."

"Yup. And you better get back this way to see us... and see that new place, too, one day soon."

Feeling emotional, I said, "I'd better hit the trail, before I start blubbering all over you guys." Not giving them time to respond, I swung up in the saddle, backed Blaze a step or two away from them, then turned her. I looked at each of them, thumbing my hat, knowing I didn't dare speak.

"Ride safe," Will said. I nodded, and headed west, with an overwhelming sense of emptiness, feeling I'd not likely see any of them again.

Eventually, we rode past the Kennedy Ranch, and I was relieved that no one was outside to see us. I didn't want to stop... to talk... to explain. Two miles beyond their place, we took the trail north. It was the same trail Mike and Sarah Jane had taken.

"Maybe we'll run into Mike one day," I told Patch. He glanced up at me, panting and smiling.

By early evening, the trail turned west, and followed a stream through a beautiful, long valley. If a man favored the solitary life, this valley would be the place to build a cabin. *Right up there on that nice plateau*, I thought. You could watch the sun rise in the morning, and set in the evening. And you'd enjoy one of the most magnificent views ever created, all day long.

Following the stream, working our way through the valley, I noticed a good place to camp for the night. Not really a cave, it was a hollowed out spot above the stream. A place where, through uncountable centuries, wind and water carved into the mountainside, leaving a rock ledge for the ceiling. Next to the hollow, there was a grassy slope where I could put Blaze.

We watched a beautiful sunset, then, with everyone fed and watered, we settled in for the night. I laid back and closed my eyes, feeling more at ease than I had in days. Turning on my side, I pulled my blanket up, and drifted into a peaceful sleep.

It was a deep, restful sleep, until... I was awakened, startled by the trembling I felt. My eyes snapped open and, for an instant, I had no idea where I was. Then things came into focus, as I recognized the hollow where we'd camped. The trembling continued and, somehow, seemed familiar.

248

I pushed myself up, and scanned the valley, dimly lit with the glow of early dawn. The stream flowed below us, splashing over scattered rocks. Everything seemed normal. Everything in its usual state. Yet my quaking continued.

I saw Blaze, head hung, eyes closed, one hind leg relaxed as she slumbered. Patch lay near me, head resting on his outstretched paws, enjoying the kind of dreams that dogs dream. The morning was fresh, cool and peacefully calm. Yet my quaking continue.

Suddenly, I had the sensation of being pulled from my body. Once again, the feeling was strangely familiar. I was rocketing upward, seeing the valley shrink in the distance below. Then, in an explosion of speed and white light, I was accelerating through time and space, bending light and distorting the dimensions.

When things finally shifted into slow motion, I found myself in a hospital bed, looking around, wondering about the tubes and monitors that I was hooked up to. There was a recliner on the other side of my bed, and Sonja lay covered in a blanket, softly sleeping. Slowly regaining my senses, I began remembering Sonja speaking with a doctor, and my thoughts of being dead.

As more of the fog cleared, I remembered a robbery, and that I'd been shot. I raised my head from the pillow, and scanned the room again. *I don't feel too bad*, I thought.

Laying my head back, I looked at Sonja and, as always, thought of how gorgeous she is. Knowing her, everything about her, made her all the more beautiful.

She stirred, slowly raising her head, and opened her eyes with a squint. "Hi Babe," I said softly.

Her eyes popped open, and she bolted upright. "Mack!" she exclaimed, in a loud, excited whisper. "Oh Mack..." she said again, scrambling from the recliner. She came close, hugged me gently, then kissed me all over my face. Finally, she pulled back, looking at me with a grin.

"Hi Babe," I repeated, softly.

"Hi there, yourself," she said. "You've been out for a couple of days now, and we've been worried sick."

"No need to worry," I told her. "They can knock me down, but not out."

"Oh you..." she said, lightly slapping my shoulder.

"Hey... hey..." I objected. "Aren't you supposed to be nice to the patient?"

She walked to the window, and opened the blinds a bit to let in the morning sun. When she turned, the sunlight caught the red tones of her beautiful auburn hair, which highlighted her striking green eyes. Again, I thought of how gorgeous she is, and how lucky I am.

"I'm a little thirsty," I whispered.

"Let me get you some fresh ice water," she said, and picked up the glass from the bedside table. She froze, staring at the glass.

"What's this?" she asked, puzzled.

"What's what?"

"This," she said, holding the glass for me to see.

250

Now I froze, feeling dumbfounded. I was staring at a bullet in the bottom of the glass. Somehow I felt I should know what... how... why... but it was lost in a fog, and I could only shrug.

Feeling a little confused, and a little empty-headed, I finally said, "Sorry Babe. I just don't know."

www.ingramcontent.com/pod-product-compliance
Lightning Source LLC
Chambersburg PA
CBHW061611170626
46811CB00001B/392